In Ruthless Pursuit

MIA MAE LYNNE

a "Southern Men Don't Fall In Love" novel

Published by: Book & Spirit, LLC

Cover Credit: Lex Hupertz

Edited by: Lex Hupertz

ISBN: 1-943651-20-5

ISBN- 978-1-943651-20-7

DEDICATION

To the almighty God of Love and Light

"Please bless this book so all readers can enjoy in the manner in which the angels and spirit guides have intended."

To my parents Johnnie Mae Parker (May 1, 1937 – April 23, 2013) and Carl Parker (April 5, 1929 – February 25, 2009)

"The lessons you gave me will follow me through eternity."

To my sons Carlos and Marcus

"Follow your dreams and the rewards will be beyond anything you can ever imagine."

To my friend Linda Smithers

"Diamonds are a girl's best friend. Your encouragement and guidance has helped me overcome seemingly impossible obstacles just by being you. You are truly my diamond."

To my friend Melissa Montgomery.

"I admire how you handle any disastrous situation with the grace and poise of the southern belle that you are. You have a gifted ability to capture the lighter side of life and spread sunshine to those who are fortunate to get to know you."

For Noel Marion, my first complete series reader

"Thank you for believing in me and taking the time to inspire me to reach for more."

For my best friend Dolphis Sloan (June 9, 1965 – February 14, 1998)

"As my big brother, you took me under your wing in my teen years and encouraged me to follow your lead in going to the University of Akron. You are a genuinely kind free spirit and even after all these years, you are still dearly missed."

ACKNOWLEDGEMENTS

"For all others who have graciously given their time to support me through the writing process, I humbly express my thanks" – Mia Mae Lynne

Kim, Dawn, Kelli & Marcella

Earth Family

Lex Hupertz

Tiffani Keaton

Nicole Penny

Mandy Varley

Nicole Westbrook

My Tribe

LIGHT WORKERS

"Light workers are those who are brought to earth and are unselfishly dedicated to giving their time to shine their light on humanity and make the world a better place." – Mia Mae Lynne

Debi J. Fellows

Spirals of Spirit, Painesville, Ohio

Effie Kapodistrias

Effie's Divine Celebration, Oakville, ON

Nicole Westbrook

Inner Fyre, Mentor, Ohio

CHAPTER 1

Carter Patrick Glass. That's what his mother called him when she wanted him to obey her wishes.

His mother wasn't here with him today, thank goodness.

She would tell him to move on.

Today was the day of the wedding.

His tuxedo was neatly pressed, hair groomed, and shoes polished. His reflection in the mirror was of a handsome brown-eyed muscular brotha with curly locks and deep dimples. The only thing missing was a smile.

He glanced at the clock and watched each passing minute as it ticked closer and closer to the Saturday nuptials. He hoped that his gaze at the clock hands would make time stand still. He dreaded the moment he had to show up at the church. He couldn't miss this wedding.

He grabbed his wallet and keys. Somehow, he made it inside of his car. He wished that he didn't have to go. He peered through the windshield, put his keys in the ignition, and started the car. He glanced over the directions to the church and returned his stare to the steering wheel.

He didn't really need the directions; he knew exactly where the church was located because he was there last night for the rehearsal. He was able to make his excuses not to stay long at the dinner but there was no excuse to keep him from going today.

As the engine revved up, he glanced over his shoulder and almost forgot to open the garage door. Quickly, he pressed the button and waited for the motor to raise the door. Daylight came suddenly. He squinted and tried to adjust to the brightness of the day.

He drove listlessly down the road.

What could he have done to change history that brought this horrific event to the reality?

This was the worst day of his life, and it had just begun.

He pulled into the church and parked his car. He watched all the happy people chatting and walking into the building. He took deep breaths and wondered how he would get through the entire ceremony without breaking down. He got out of the car. It was difficult for him to fake happiness when he was depressed. He passed several guests, greeted them and walked up the steps to the church. He found the room for the groom and his men.

***

He stood at the altar and felt his imminent doom. His heart raced while he waited for the bride to appear.

She entered and the room became too warm. Her veil covered her smiling, sweet, tawny brown face. The pink and green flowers of her bouquet rested on her arm with delicate grace. The soft white wedding gown fitted her body and showed each curve in a bold but respectful way. She clutched her father's arm, took slow deliberate steps, and walked closer and closer to the altar.

His heart told him to break down and stop this farce, and his mind told him that it was too late. For once, his mind was right, and he remained silent even when the pastor asked if anyone had reason to object to the marriage.

Hell yeah he objected. He was in love with the bride and she didn't know it.

Terri was his ideal woman and she was making a big mistake.

He stood there, listened to the pastor and repeated Ricky's vows in his head. He wished he were the man making a lifetime commitment to her. Ricky had no clue that he was marrying the woman of Carter's dreams.

He'd better take good care of her.

Carter would make sure of that.

She'd made her choice and Carter never said a word. He allowed Terri to see Ricky without interference and thought she'd see right through the player, but he never thought Ricky would propose and she would accept.

When Terri and Ricky announced their engagement at a family picnic, he was speechless. They assumed that it was the silence of happiness. Carter felt the nails in his coffin suffocating him. He'd managed a polite "Congratulations."

Now, at the altar, watching another man take the woman he should have stepped to first, Carter prayed that the minister finished this farce soon.

As he witnessed the kiss of the bride and groom, he moistened his lips and envisioned what it would be like if she were wrapped in his arms and this was their day together.

The cheers and movement of the bride and groom towards the entrance of the church were his cue to step back to the reality of the wedding.

He offered his arm to the bridesmaid next to him. He couldn't shake the empty feeling of missing the love of his life. A woman who would never knew how he felt. She was unavailable, married to his good friend. He hoped that no one knew his agony, that no one could read it in his face.

He stood motionless at the top of the stairs to the church. The guests strolled past him, chatted, and hugged in celebration of the newlywed couple. He was oblivious to the gaiety as he was still mulling over his cowardice to take what he wanted and now would never have.

"We're supposed to be in the pictures." Maya said. The bridesmaid gave Carter a gentle smile, and he tried to return the expression.

"Yea, okay."

"Everyone is waiting for you." Maya said.

"I'm coming."

He followed her into the church and took his place amongst the bridal party for the pictures that would be reminders of his day of despair. He was coaxed by the photographer to smile for the camera and he did just enough not to ruin the photos. The heavy burden in his heart made his chest hurt. Somehow his heart kept beating. The ticking off each second of time from the moment that he'd lost his true love to another man.

He took a seat on a pew and watched Terri and Ricky take more pictures, lavishing in their attention for the day. If only he could turn back the hands of time, he would be next to Terri and they would be starting their life together, but fate had chosen another course.

The heat of the church, the racing of his heart and the trembling of his hands forced him to rise suddenly from his seat. Quickly, he walked down the aisle towards the door and made a mad dash for the haven of his car.

He started the engine and rolled down the windows so as not to suffocate himself. He exhaled and wiped the sweat off his brow.

No excuses.

He had to attend the reception as part of his duties. No one said that he had to be there right now.

He leaned back in his seat.

The knock on the passenger side window startled him.

"Can I ride with you to the reception?"

"Sure, Maya, get in."

"Thanks, Carter."

CHAPTER 2

The ride was quiet.

Maya took in the scenery and watched out the window while he drove to the reception with the urgency of a fast-moving tortoise. Maya let out a sneeze and shattered the peacefulness of the calm.

"Bless you."

"Thanks."

"Did you enjoying the wedding?" he asked.

Maya gripped the flowers on her lap. She wistfully answered, "I did. Terri was beautiful."

He drew a sigh and wished she hadn't said that. "She did look beautiful." Carter signaled to change lanes. "Pink is a good color for you."

Maya blushed. "Thank you, you didn't have to say that. I know I'm not as attractive as my cousins."

He laughed. "Don't sell yourself short."

"You're a good friend to have. You always seem to know what to say."

He acknowledged her statement and continued his drive to get the last part of this day over.

MIA MAE LYNNE

They arrived at the reception twenty minutes late. Terri's sister, Lisa, approached them.

"Where have you been? Everyone's waiting for you."

"Traffic," he said unapologetically. "We're here now. What do we have to do?"

They followed Lisa to sit with the bridal party. The meal was being served and Carter took his seat. He picked at the chicken and green beans. The potatoes weren't bad, but everything tasted more like ash in his mouth than food.

Surrounded by everyone's joy at the happy couple was making him sick at heart. He lowered his eyes in silent prayer to hold his emotions together.

His pain was far greater than their joy.

Ricky's brother Gerald stood up to make the toast.

"We never thought that we would see this day come. My brother, Ricky, is a man motivated by inspiration. Mom always inspired him to do well in school. I inspired him to do well in sports but there was something missing. Ricky searched continuously to find the woman who could inspire him and push him to excel beyond his comfort zone.

"When he met Terri, we knew that he found his inspiration to be a better man and become one with

God. Terri, we welcome you into our family and into our hearts. May God bless this union forever. Amen."

Carter rose from his chair and clasped Ricky's shoulder. He extended his hand. "Congratulations, Frat. You're one lucky man and you know it."

Ricky shook his hand with a firm grip. "Thanks, man. I'm glad that you're here."

"Wouldn't have missed it for my brother." Carter managed to voice the lie without throwing up. "I wish you and Terri the best."

Carter returned to his chair. He stared out into the crowd of happy faces, his lips pressed tight together and throat parched. He reached for his glass of wine at the same time his seatmate did. The cool rush of liquid on his pants made him jump from his seat.

"Oh, Carter, I'm sorry."

He rushed to get a napkin to wipe his pants.

Maya continued to apologize. "I didn't mean to do that, Carter. Clumsy, I guess."

"No worries, Maya."

"May I ask you something?"

"What's that?"

"Have you ever been so in love with someone, but they've never even noticed you?"

Carter was floored. .

Yes, he knew that feeling exactly

"Take the chance and talk to him, Maya." He added under his breath, "Otherwise, she'll be dancing at her wedding with someone else."

Maya blushed, shook her head. "I don't think I can risk that."

***

The music began after everyone finished eating. Ricky stood up and led Terri to the dance floor.

Carter watched her from a distance during the entire reception and couldn't keep his eyes away from her.

Several of the male guests were invited to dance with the bride and Carter purposely stayed away from Terri.

When it was time for the garter toss, he excused himself and hid in the men's room.

Ricky's friend, Chris, caught the garter of doom.

Carter's bride had just married another man. He wasn't ever getting married, garter or no.

He mingled with several of the guests and hoped that he could be distracted enough to tell his heart to move on.

When midnight approached, he eased his way to the door. Just as he was about to slip out quietly, someone tapped his shoulder. He turned.

"Thank you for being in our wedding."

He was too mesmerized for words. Terri was standing in front of him in all white, newly married to another man. She extended her arms for a hug.

Didn't she know that it was dangerous to hug a man that wasn't her husband? Especially one who was in love with her?

He warmly accepted her gesture, closed his eyes, and allowed his thoughts to take him anywhere but here.

He couldn't look at her in the eyes because he was afraid that she would read his mind. He didn't want his emotions to show so he quickly released her and wished her well.

Ricky stood beside her, took her hand, and led her away.

Carter watched the pair stop at a table to socialize with an elder guest.

This was no place for him to be.

He left the room as quickly as possible and made it to the safety of his car.

He drove his black Honda Accord away from the reception and hoped to put distance between him, the wedding, and his feelings for Terri.

CHAPTER 3

"Party time."

He pulled out his dress clothes and laid them across the bed. It was time for him to get out of the house for the evening and do some socializing. His friend, Greg, was in town and loved to party. A lot of their peers were settling down with families or serious girlfriends. Greg loved to play the field and Carter was his riding buddy.

He expected Greg to call to finalize their plans for the evening. When the phone rang, he answered to his mother's voice instead. "How's my boy?"

"I'm fine. I'm going out with Greg in a few. Is everything alright in Twinsburg?" he grabbed his wallet and threw it on the bed. He'd just stepped out of the shower and was splashing on his favorite aftershave.

"I won't keep you. I can't wait to see you for Christmas. We remodeled the basement."

"That's great, Mom. I love you. I have to get ready to leave. Greg will be here any minute."

As soon as he hung up the phone, his doorbell rang. He threw on a robe, rushed down the hall, and answered the door.

Greg Speaks raised his eyebrows with a grin before stepping across the threshold into Carter's house. "Dog, I hope you're not going like that?"

"Nah, man," Carter laughed. "I'm running late. Give me a few. I'm almost set."

Ten minutes later, Carter was ready to leave. Greg left the house first. Carter locked up and noticed a new hunter green Jaguar in his driveway. Greg stood next to it with an elated expression.

"It must be nice." Carter teased.

Greg's smile broadened, pleased that his friend noticed his new car.

"You like it?"

"Yea, it's cool."

"Hop in."

They arrived at Shea's Nightclub and walked through the door together. Carter saw a familiar face across the room.

Greg elbowed Carter, gaze drawn to the same scene he was watching of Ricky flirting with the women around his table.

"Did you see that?" Greg asked. "This is why I don't come to black clubs. His ass just got married and he's still looking for more pussy. He's going to get busted. All sistahs know each other."

Carter sucked in his cheeks and clenched his teeth. He couldn't believe what he saw either. The women were flocking to Ricky and he was lavishing in the attention. Ricky should be home in bed with his woman. Why the hell did he get married if he wasn't planning on playing the field?

"Yea, I see it." Carter responded slowly.

"What do you want to do?"

Carter shrugged. "It's none of our business."

I'd like to punch his ass out.

"He's frat so we're under G-code, but he's your friend."

The code of honor.

The unwritten rules that separate men from boys.

Rule #6 - Never bust a playa in his game.

"I'll be right back." Carter walked over to Ricky and Greg followed him.

Ricky was making false promises that Carter knew he couldn't keep to his new girlfriends. The brotha was digging his grave.

"What's up, frat?" Ricky stood up and gave Carter the grip.

Greg extended his hand as well.

"Just hanging with some honeys," he said and stepped away from the table to talk to them.

Ricky stared Carter in the eyes. "G-code."

Carter felt his stomach tighten and anger blazed in his chest. This wasn't the place to make a scene or jump to conclusions.

"Handle your business," Carter said and glared at him. "Do right by your wife."

"Noted dog. It's all good." Ricky stated. "Come join us for drinks."

"It is." Greg said. "We'll come back later. I know a few friends that I've got to introduce to Carter. He's into black women and I know a few he could sing to that would throw their panties at him."

Ricky doubled over and laughed. "Alright playas. Get your groove on and I'm going to get mine. We'll speak soon."

Greg nudged Carter and they walked away.

"Thanks for the save."

"Any time bro'. I know you're not into white girls, but I've got this top forty place we can chill at for an hour or so. I know you don't approve of what he's doing. If we stay, we might not like what else we see."

"Agreed. Let's get out of here."

He felt strange leaving Ricky with those women and was very concerned about Terri. He wanted to warn her because he cared for her. He couldn't call this late in the evening and he couldn't stop by. He wondered how he could help Terri see that Ricky was no good for her, without her wondering why he hadn't said anything before.

CHAPTER 4

He came home around 4:00 p.m. Saturday afternoon after refereeing a few basketball games. He grabbed a beer from the fridge and sat down on the recliner. He placed his beer on the coaster, picked up his cellphone.

She called?

I have to listen to her message.

"Hi Carter, call me. I need a favor. Talk soon! And thanks in advance!"

He felt a tightness in his chest when he heard her voice. He tried to forget her eyes, her scent, and her smile when she met his gaze.

He played the message again just to hear that she needed him.

He didn't know what the favor was but would do anything that Terri asked. He stared at the phone in his hand, wondered if he should call now. She could be planning her evening out.

He punched in the digits by memory.

"This is Terri."

"It's Carter. You called."

He imagined he heard a catch in her breath before she responded. "I did. Brenda and I are looking for a bartender for a private party at the Brimmer's house. Can you come?"

What luck.

Terri called him and required his assistance. This would give him a chance to be near her with a valid excuse. He checked his calendar to make sure he could be there. If there was anything on his calendar, he'd cancel it. "Sure. I'll be there. Give me all of the information."

"Great! Thank you so much. Let's meet for coffee and we can discuss the details."

***

He was on his way to the Atlanta Bread Company in Roswell to meet Terri to review the details for the Brimmer party.

When he opened the door to the coffee shop, he saw her seated at a table near the window with a cup of coffee and a book in her hand. Her hair was down and she wore round dark rimmed glasses.

She eagerly waved at him.

He walked over to the table.

She stood up and hugged him. He wrapped his arm around her waist and brought her close to him.

She kissed his cheek, undoubtedly leaving a lipstick imprint, which he welcomed, especially from her.

"I'll grab some coffee and come back. Do you want anything?"

"I'll have a refill," she answered.

After he brought back the drinks, he removed his coat and sat across from her.

"What's up? When you called to meet for coffee, it sounded important like there was more on your mind than just the party."

"There is." She closed her book and placed it in her paisley satchel bag. "I want your opinion on something."

"I'm listening."

"I'm thinking about quitting my job and starting a full-time catering business."

Carter's smile widened across his face. "Do the damn thing. Tell me about it."

Terri had hinted at owning her own business over the past year. He was confident that it would be well run. She paid close attention to the small details.

"I want to get a small business loan and open up a café in Roswell that also does catering. I haven't told Ricky yet." Her eyes lowered, and he heard the sadness in her voice. "I'm not sure he understands my dream. He wants me to work at my job and do catering on the side. I want to be independent." She sighed.

He reached across the table and placed his hand over hers. "I'll support your dream. If you need a financial backer, attorney, or an accountant, let me know."

She removed her hand from under his and picked up her coffee cup. "Thank you. Lisa will help me with the accounting and Doug's an attorney. I wanted to talk to you to see if you would continue to help me with the parties. Ricky doesn't know how to bartend, and I can't seem to get him involved in my dream."

He pulled his hand back from the table, picked up his cup and took a sip.

Maybe I moved too fast?

"This doesn't sound right. Your man should back you in your dreams. How's married life treating you? I want you to be happy."

Her eyes watered, and she took a deep breath. She sipped her coffee and evaded eye contact. "It'll get better."

I hope not. Leave that brother and marry me.

She took a deep breath, forced a smile on her face and looked in his eyes. "By the way, thank you for stepping in as the keyboardist for Lisa's wedding. I know it's last minute and all."

Carter nodded. "No problem." *I would do anything for you.*

"By the way, I have a friend that's single. I think the two of you would look cute together. Her name is Charlene. Do you want her number?"

Carter laughed. "Not right now."

"Okay," she laughed. "You have the worst taste in women. I was glad when you broke up with Cynthia. I didn't like her. You deserve better."

"Like who?" he asked. *You're unavailable.* "I'm leaving my options open. My Nubian queen isn't available yet."

Terri's eyes widened. "She isn't? You have someone in mind." She laughed. "Should I be jealous? You're not going to bartend for someone else, are you?" At least she was smiling again, eyes no longer on the brink of tears. "Tell me about her."

If you only knew. I'm looking right at her. "No one in particular."

"Well," Terri put down her coffee and twisted the wedding ring around her finger, "if you haven't met her then you need to go out. I'm sure there are plenty of places to meet someone. If you don't like Charlene, I have other girlfriends I could introduce to you."

He stared at the ring and felt pangs of jealousy in the pit of his stomach. His perfect woman married his frat brother who wasn't treating her well.

"Why are you trying to fix me up? What's wrong with being a bachelor?" he asked.

She blushed. "I think you're a great guy and a good friend. Why wouldn't I want you to have your Nubian queen? I have so many girlfriends that can't find the right guy."

And you didn't either. You settled for a cheater.

"About Charlene—"

He held up his hand and halted her. "When I find the right woman, I hope she's a lot like you." He stood up and kissed her on the cheek. "I have to go. My sister needs me to watch her kids."

"Oh, okay. See you later, Carter. Thanks for being available to help at the party."

"Always for you, Terri. See you then."

CHAPTER 5

Carter opened his front door late Friday evening. His niece, Shante, and nephew, Kinte, burst through the door right past him. They argued with each other over who would get to watch the TV first.

His sister, Joy, yelled at the kids. "Stop it and give me the remote."

Shante snatched the remote out of Kinte's hands, marched over to her mother, and gave it to her.

Joy frowned, shook her head, and handed the remote to her brother. "I'm sorry about that, Boo-boo. Are you sure you can handle them for an overnight stay?"

"I got this." Carter said, smiling at the kids. "The two of you will be here all night but I get first dibs on my own TV."

"Uncle Boo-boo..." Shante whined.

"Don't call me that." Carter said sternly. "Only my mother and my sisters call me that. I'm Uncle Carter."

"But *Are you Afraid of the Dark* is on!" Shante whined.

"Shante, stop it. You just got here, spend time with your uncle." Joy glared at her daughter.

Carter laughed, rolling his eyes at the children and their mother. "Go and have a good time tonight." He held the door and waved his sister out. "I can handle the kids, but remember I have plans tomorrow so make sure you come and get them before lunch. I have to help cater a party."

"Oh yea sure. I'll get them early."

He knew his sister. If he didn't give her a time, he'd be stuck with the kids all weekend.

"I'll be back with their bags." She rushed to the car and returned to the house with two duffel bags.

"Call mamma if you need anything."

"Bye, sis."

He closed the door and watched Joy pull out of the driveway.

She'd confided in him earlier that she had a date for dinner and breakfast. It was hard for her to have private time with kids around.

Before he could say anything further to the kids, his cell phone rang. He scampered to find it in the kitchen. He recognized the number and picked it up before it rang a third time. "Hey Ricky. What's going on?"

"It's not Ricky. It's Terri."

He paused at hearing her voice. His beauty needed him. Whatever she wanted, he was ready to do it.

"What time are you coming over tomorrow? I thought Ricky would be back home but he's still out of town. I can't lift everything myself. Can you help? I'll make you lunch!"

Carter laughed; unable to help the surge of male pride at being the one she called to bail her out of a jam. "Sure. I'll be over around noon."

The words escaped his mouth before he thought about it. He was treading on thin ice by going over to Terri's house with her man out of town.

He hoped his sister would be on time to get her kids.

"You're a godsend. Thank you. I'll see you tomorrow."

"See you then."

He took a deep breath and hung up.

God must have had a sense of humor teasing him with a woman he couldn't have.

How am I going to keep my feelings hidden from her?

He looked down at both his niece and nephew.

They stared at him.

"Who was that?" Shante asked.

"Is she pretty?"

"Is she your girlfriend?"

"Enough! Just go watch TV," he said.

Shante grinned and Kinte crossed his arms over his chest. "You've got the remote."

The beginnings of a headache began to stir behind his eyes.

Two kids. A woman who needed him. And a whole lot of trouble if her man caught him with Terri.

The kids he could at least take care of.

"This is the plan. Shante, you have the TV in my bedroom for an hour. Kinte and I will be out here watching TV. We'll get pizza and salad for dinner then maybe watch a movie afterwards."

"Thank you, Uncle Carter." Both kids hugged him.

***

One soft touch of her hand caressed his chest. She stroked his inner thigh; her head nestled on his shoulder.

Her lips pressed against his neck.

His lips covered over hers. He inhaled her breath into every cell of his body. His hands tangled in her soft and beautiful hair.

His wrapped his arms around her, pulled her against his body. Her nipples pressed into him. She clutched at his shoulders.

Her legs wrapped around his waist and he thrust— "You spilled it all over the floor. Uncle Carter's going to get you."

"You snatched it from me."

"No, I didn't!"

"Yes, you did."

Carter woke from his sleep and having forgotten that he had his niece and nephew overnight. He should've been up earlier.

Those two were a handful.

"Ugh."

He threw his feet over the side of the bed and glanced at the clock. It was 9:00 a.m. and he'd promised to be at Terri's by lunchtime.

"Quiet down in there." He yelled.

The kids stopped arguing and knocked on the door. He picked up his pants from the side of the bed and put them on. He opened his door.

"Kinte spilled Captain Crunch all over your floor."

"No, I didn't. She snatched it from me then it spilled."

"Both of you will clean it up. Go. I'll follow you."

The kids ran to the kitchen.

As soon as he stepped on the tile, his bare feet felt the scratchy cereal.

He stared at them.

They stared back.

Silence.

He marched over to the closet and smashed a few more pieces along the way. He pulled out a broom and handed it to Shante. He reached for the dustpan and gave it to Kinte.

"Clean it up, now. There will be no fighting. When I get back from calling your mother, I expect this kitchen to be swept."

He went back to his bedroom and picked up the phone. There wasn't any more arguing to be heard from the kitchen. He dialed Joy.

No answer.

Where the hell was she?

He went back to the kitchen and both kids were seated at the table. "Did you eat?"

"Yes, Uncle Carter." They both answered.

"Go wash up and get dressed. Your mother wasn't home, but you need to be ready when she gets here. Shante you use the guest bathroom. I'll send your brother to my bathroom."

"Yes, Uncle Carter." Shante darted out of the room.

"Grab your stuff my man and get dressed." Kinte left the kitchen, found his duffel and occupied Carter's bathroom.

While the kids were gone, he brewed a pot of coffee. He poured a cup, sat down at the table, and picked up the paper from the day before.

On the headline on the newspaper was the trial of a local woman who shot her husband. She caught him in her bed with another woman.

Damn!

What if Terri caught Ricky in the middle of his shenanigans?

Would she shoot him?

He saw his phone, reached across the table, and grabbed it. He called Joy again.

"Hi, Boo-boo."

"Where are you? I need you to pick up the kids. I've got someplace to go."

"I'm at the hairdresser. I'm not sure how long this will take. Can you watch them a little while longer for me?"

No! He had to be with Terri.

"I can't. I've got another commitment."

"Please. For me. I don't get a chance to get my hair done often. I can't get anyone to watch them. You're my only hope."

He couldn't say no to her, which was always his problem. "Okay just tell your slow beautician to stop running her mouth and hurry up."

Joy giggled. "I want my hair to look good. You can't rush beauty."

"I know." He smiled despite himself, glad he could at least help one lady out. "I'm playing with you. Love you, Sis."

Damn!

He hung up the phone and knew he was on the hook for at least another three to four hours. A sistah could be in the beauty shop all day.

Now that his time with the kids extended past lunch, he wasn't sure what to do about his plans with Terri.

Call her anyway.

Just as he was about to press a digit, the phone rang. "Hi, Carter. Are you coming over?"

He hesitated. "I have my niece and nephew. My sister had some unexpected things to come up, so I don't know when I'll be over."

"Why don't you bring them with you?" she suggested.

Perfect. "I'll be over in an hour."

CHAPTER 6

Carter arrived at Terri's home. She opened the door and welcomed him in. first Terri.

"I'm Shante and this is my brother, Kinte. Where's your bathroom?"

Carter put his hand on her shoulder. "Shante, slow your roll."

"That's okay," Terri laughed. "I'll show her where it is."

Terri directed Shante to the guest bathroom and then beckoned Kinte and Carter to follow her to the kitchen. It was filled with pans on the counters covered in aluminum foil. She opened the oven and the smell of blueberry infused the air and reached the pit of Carter's empty stomach.

"Do you need any help?" he offered.

"I have it. Thanks." She removed the pie from the oven before taking off her mitts, and putting them on the counter.

Shante burst into the kitchen and stood in front of Terri. "Well your bathroom gets a rating of a seven. Your towels aren't clean, you don't have enough toilet paper, and one of your lights is out."

Carter inhaled a deep breath and sighed. This would be a long afternoon with his outspoken niece. His cheeks hardened, and he pressed his lips together tight. "Shante—"

Terri laughed and broke the tension. "There's more toilet paper under the sink; I can get some fresh towels, and I didn't realize that the bathroom light was out. Normally, my husband uses that one but he must not have realized the light was out."

Shante looked ready to throw another tirade before Kinte interrupted: "I'm thirsty."

"I'll get you something to drink." Terri pulled out a pitcher of iced tea and served everyone a glass. She removed four plates from the cupboard and prepared lunch for everyone from the food she'd catered for that evening's party.

Shante scooted in her chair, licked her fingers, and wiped her face with the back of her hands. The sticky barbecue sauce smeared across her face. "Miss Terri, this chicken is good. Who taught you how to cook?"

Terri reached across the table and wiped Shante's face with a wet towel. Carter smiled and nodded at Terri's gesture. He loved how she mothered his niece.

Terri responded. "My mother. All the women in my family had to learn how to cook from the age of seven."

A smile beamed across Shante's face, "I'll be seven on Christmas Day. Will you teach me how to cook like this?"

"I will with your mother's permission." Terri answered.

Carter interjected. "I'm sure she won't mind. I'll bring you over."

Terri pushed her chair back from the table, collected her plate and placed it in the sink. She picked up the list off the counter. "Two trays mashed potatoes, three trays of chicken…"

Before he could volunteer to help, his phone rang.

"Hi, Sis."

"I'll be home in twenty minutes."

"All right. We'll finish up here and be right over."

***

Now, heading back to help Terri with any last-minute chores, Carter looked over at the surprise on his seat with a smile.

Just something small, to make her feel special.

She answered the door. "You're back. That was fast."

He stepped over the threshold and handed her the gift. "For you."

She narrowed her eyes. "For me?" She removed the paper and gasped. It was a large wooden plaque inscribed with her business name, "Terri's Tasty Treats and Eats"

"I wanted to bring you something to inspire you."

She put the plaque down, pulled his face to hers and kissed him closed mouth tightly on the lips. "Thank you. You have no idea how much this means to me."

Taken aback by the unexpected gratitude, he stepped back to give them distance just in case her husband was home. "You're welcome."

"I applied for my business license. I'm working on my small business loan. I'll start looking for locations soon." She gripped the plaque tightly. "I'll put this up in the dining room of my restaurant."

"Let me know. I'm here if you need me."

Terri's eyes filled with sadness. "I'm not sure when that will happen. Ricky and I are arguing over it. It's as if he doesn't want me to fulfill my dreams. He thinks that security is having a forty hour a week job and has no sense of entrepreneurship or being self-employed."

"I'll do anything you want me to do including bartending. I love you. Eh. I mean love to help you fulfill your dreams," he stated.

"Thank you." She smiled. "You've been a great friend."

"Now tell me what you need me to do."

"Well," she stammered, "I could really use some help doing dishes."

"Sure. I'm great with a sponge."

He went to the kitchen, filled the dishpan with water and soaked the silverware. He washed a large roaster and she grabbed it to dry.

She smiled at him when he handed her a platter.

"I apologize for Shante's behavior," he said.

"She's very outspoken." She dried the platter, put it away, and went to take out the garbage.

"Stop," he ordered. "I'll get that."

Was it just him, or did she shiver when he said that? When he reached around her to take out the trash for her?

"Thank you," she said.

"My pleasure." He took out the bag. I keep the kids for my sister when she needs me. Her ex-boyfriends aren't around much."

"That's thoughtful of you," her eyes glistened with admiration. "You must be close to your family."

He laughed. "I'm the only son and my sisters call me all the time. I'm surprised my phone hasn't rang this morning. My oldest sister, Kim fills me in on the family gossip. It must be quiet this weekend."

She lightly brushed her hand down his shirtsleeve. "It's getting late and I'll have to change soon. Are you wearing that?"

"No. I'll run by the house and meet you at the Brimmer's."

She took his hands into hers and gazed into his eyes. "It's been really nice having you around."

His heart beat faster. He lowered his eyes to hers. "It's nice to be needed." Their lips drifted towards each other. She took a step back and looked around the kitchen. His shoulders slumped when she pulled away.

"Well," she sighed, "I think we're almost done here."

"Are we?" he tilted his head and squeezed her hands.

"Eh, yea," she breathed. "We are. Carter I —"

The phone rang.

"I need to get that."

His smiled and let her go. "I'll finish packing the utensils."

The phone continued to ring but neither one moved to answer it.

She took a deep breath, exhaled, and murmured. "That may have been Ricky."

"I guess you should call him back," he said softy.

"Yea. Yes!" She blinked her eyes and jerked her shoulders back. "I should. Brenda should be here any minute." She released his hands and walked past him to look for the phone.

"It's on the table." Carter called out.

She returned to the kitchen and sheepishly responded, "Thanks. I'm not sure where my mind is right now."

I hope it's on me.

The doorbell rang and Terri left the kitchen, opened the door, and laughed loud enough that Carter heard her from his place by the oven. "What are you doing here? Did you get a hall pass from Mr. Doug?"

"Shut up," responded a voice.

Carter entered the living room to see who was at the door.

Terri hugged her sister.

"Not so tight my breasts are sore—" Lisa paused and looked at Carter.

Terri turned around and smiled. "You remember my sister, right, Carter?"

He smiled. "Of course. How are you?" He embraced her lightly. "How's Doug?"

"Crazy as ever. I came by for a few minutes to get a break. I want to sample some of the chicken wings Terri made. I can't take them home."

Terri laughed. "We're still cleaning up. Come into the kitchen."

They moved to the kitchen and Lisa took a chair at the table.

Terri grabbed a plate and served her sister a few wings. She brushed her hand down Carter's arm as she passed. "Will you please finish the big pots for me?

He smiled and winked at her. "Sure." He grabbed a dishrag and filled the dishpan with fresh water.

"He's very attentive." Lisa said. "I didn't know you had two husbands." Terri and Carter laughed.

"Only one and that's plenty." Terri said and winked at Carter.

"I think I like this one better than the other." Lisa said under her breath, still loud enough for Carter to hear it.

"Hush," Terri scolded. She grinned when she met Carter's stare over the counter. "Bigamy isn't legal in Georgia."

Carter laughed.

If she only knew…

Terri picked up a dishtowel and dried the roaster. "I'm going to introduce him to Charlene."

Lisa shook her head. "Stop playing match maker. He's not interested in Charlene. You know no one is interested in that sistah."

Terri waved her hand to and shook her head to stop her sister from speaking further. "Cut it out, Lisa. Besides, all of Carter's frat brothers are getting married. He needs a wife just like Ricky needs me."

"I don't know why you married that idiot," Lisa said and glanced over at Carter. "I'll change the subject since we have a third-party spy from the man camp."

"I didn't hear a word." Carter smirked and lifted the lever on the faucet to rinse a few pans and drown out some of the conversation.

CHAPTER 7

When he pulled in the driveway to the Brimmer's lake house, his eyes zeroed in on Terri. She leaned over to pick up a box and he rolled down the window to call after her.

"I can get that after I park. Don't worry about it."

Terri looked up and smiled at him, brushing back a hank of hair that had fallen into her eyes with a relieved grin. "Thank you, Carter. Just in time, as always."

He parked the car, approached her and swept the box off the ground. She gave him a half hug. He leaned sideways and placed his cheek next to hers.

She pulled away and motioned to the woman next to her. "This is Brenda."

"Hello." The woman had striking short blonde hair against her dark brown skin. "Nice to meet you. I'll see both of you inside." Brenda took a tray covered with aluminum foil inside of the house.

Terri circled the back of the van and grabbed a similar tray. "All your errands run? You're just in time for the event to start. Let me show you to the bar."

He followed her inside the house to the entertainment room.

It had a long wood bar with six stools.

Ten tables were set up with decorations on the cherry hardwood floor.

He assessed the inventory and was impressed with the stock of premium alcohol, wine, and beer.

"The Brimmer family is in the pet care industry. There'll be several executives and their spouses. Don't serve anyone that appears to be intoxicated. Call me if you have any problems. Mrs. Brimmer can call a cab for anyone that wants a safe ride home."

He listened to the words flow through her lightly painted lips. Her dark brown hair laid softly against her skin and her almond shaped eyes were perfectly lined and mascaraed under her eyebrows.

Every time he looked at her was like falling in love all over again.

"I'll remember that." He whispered his answer in a slow and intense voice, wanting to savor the moment between them.

She caught his gaze before she abruptly turned and walked away with long deliberate strides.

He wanted her.

It wasn't going to happen.

"Ahem."

Brenda took a seat at the bar and scowled at him.

"Can I help you?"

She lifted her forefinger and waved her shiny navy acrylic nail at him, "Stay out of trouble."

"I don't understand." He faced her and wiped away any expression on his face.

She blinked her eyes and extended her neck forward. "I think you do. Only a blind bat can't see that you're in love with her."

He pressed his lips tight and responded with a deep growl. "Mind your business, Brenda."

"Ricky'll figure it out."

He stepped back from the bar, picked up a glass, and filled it with ice. Brenda wasn't going to ruin his chances of spending time with Terri even if it was only for an evening. "Don't start none won't be none, Brenda. What else can I help you with?"

"Just take care of our guests. I'll check on you later." Brenda stood up and swiftly left the bar.

If a nosy woman like Brenda could see how he felt, then why didn't Terri know it?

***

It was 1:30 a.m. when he glanced at the clock. The last few guests were saying their goodbyes. He'd been successful in making a few new business contacts and possibly more moonlighting as a bartender.

He wiped down the last barstool and grabbed his coat.

Terri approached him.

"Can you drop me off at home? Brenda brought me, and she left an hour ago. I can't get a hold of Ricky to pick me up."

What luck. A damsel in distress by her no-good husband.

Knowing Ricky, he was under some hoochie mama getting his rocks off, expecting to come home late and Terri not to notice.

This brother left his territory open to invasion and Carter was available to take care of her needs.

"Sure, I'll take you home. Let me know when you're ready to go."

***

They were five minutes away from the Brimmer's estate when he put in some soft jazz to lighten the mood of the busy evening. He was thankful that it was dark outside because the peaceful grin plastered on his face would've been met with questions.

One day she will be mine.

All mine.

She leaned on the car door and placed her hands over her forehead. She shifted in her seat and opened her eyes slightly. "I'm sorry that I'm not much company."

"Get your rest. It's cool," he responded.

"Where are we?" she yawned and sat up.

"Not far from your house. How's your family?"

She stretched her neck and rolled her shoulders, "Everyone's doing fine. Lisa and Doug are hosting Christmas dinner. Ricky and Doug don't like each other so we have to keep them apart. My parents are doing okay."

He wasn't interested in hearing about what Ricky liked. He wanted Ricky to seal the deal and leave Terri.

"I saw you talking to Jay Brimmer," she teased. "He likes you."

He grinned. "The Brimmer's have a nice crib. Jay Brimmer is a friend of Noel. She owns Noel's House of Jazz."

"Hey, I didn't know that. I love that place. Have you been there?" she asked

He nodded. "Yea, it's a cool place."

"I'll have to take Ricky sometime."

Now why did she have to go and say that?

Rub salt into an old wound that refused to let her go.

He pulled into her driveway and dreaded that their time was ended. "Yea, you'll have to do that."

Terri gathered her belongings from the backseat of the car and Carter walked her to the door.

"I don't think he's home," she lamented. She placed her key in the door and the only light on in the house was the one in the foyer.

"Where do you want me to put your things?" he asked and stepped inside the house.

"Here. I'll put them away later."

He placed her belongings on the floor as not to block the doorway.

She brushed her hand against his sleeve and looked up into his eyes. "Thanks for everything, Carter. You don't know how much this means to me."

"You're welcome," he spoke in a half-whispered tone. "It will get better. I promise."

She circled her arms around his waist and hugged him tight. "I'm just so tired."

He lifted his hands and wasn't sure what to do with them. If he wrapped them around her, he wouldn't let her go and this wasn't the time or place to express his feelings towards her. She really needed a friend.

He lowered his lips and softly pressed them against her forehead. "I have to go. It will work out."

CHAPTER 8

Relaxed on the couch in front of the TV Saturday evening, Carter's phone rang and shook him out of his light slumber.

"What's up?" He answered and paused the TV.

"My boy, I'm in town. Let's go club hopping." Greg said excitedly through the phone.

"Time?"

"I'll be there in a couple of hours. Go back and get your beauty sleep. Be ready at nine."

"Yo, okay." Carter hung up the phone and wiped the sleep from his eyes.

Might as well get up or he'd still be on the couch when Greg got there.

***

"All set?" Greg asked as Carter got into the jag.

"Yea, man. Let's do it." Carter squeezed his cheeks hard to force a wide grin across his face. He wasn't interested in meeting anyone, but it was better than staying at home.

"The Breeze Point should be hopping tonight."

"Man, I've never heard of that place."

"It's new." Greg chuckled and pulled out of the driveway.

"What's new with Bambi? I thought you'd be somewhere with her tonight."

"She's busy visiting family."

"So, you got the night off?"

"Absolutely."

They arrived at the top forty club, which had a long line of people waiting to get in. Carter surveyed his surroundings of the majority crowd, and majority meant all white.

Ten minutes later, they moved their way through the crowd and found an empty table. Greg winked at a couple of women and asked them to join him and Carter at the table.

"Hi. I'm Sara and this is Debbie."

"Hi guys." Debbie said.

"I'm Greg, and this is Carter."

"Nice to meet you." Carter extended his hand to both women.

Sara, the brown-haired woman, sat next to Greg. He waived down a tall thin blonde server to come to the table.

"Anything to drink?" the server asked.

"I got this round." Greg flashed his platinum credit card and smiled at the women sitting with them. "Ladies please give her your order."

Everyone ordered.

Greg whispered in Sara's ear and they left to party on the dance floor

Carter was left with Debbie. Although it was dark, he could tell that she was a redhead. The white sparkled top she wore was cut low with her breasts pushed up and squeezed together. His eyes lowered below her neck to see what else was revealed.

Yep, stuck with the Bimbo. He quickly lifted his eyes to meet hers.

"So, what's your profession?" She asked and brushed her hair off her shoulders.

"I'm a purchasing manager at Parker Logistics."

"Sounds intense. I'm a pharmacist."

A pharmacist?

She can't be that smart.

The server returned with the drinks, which he readily accepted and took a swallow, feeling the burn as it went down his throat.

"We should go out sometime." She flashed him a smile and winked.

How about never?

"I'll let you know. My schedule is hectic." He stood up and stepped back from the table.

"Where are you going?" she said with a puzzled expression. "You haven't finished your drink."

"I have to make some calls."

Carter moved his way through the crowd to a clearing in the hall away from the blaring music. He wished that he'd driven separately from Greg. He hadn't been in the mood to socialize and thought that getting out of the house would help his mood, but he'd been wrong.

He felt a tug on his sleeve.

"I know you're not leaving. I've got the keys to the ride." Greg laughed.

Carter shrugged his shoulders unapologetically. "I just needed some air. This isn't my crowd."

"What do you mean? The place is packed. Lots of action here."

"You know what I mean. Ain't enough sistahs in this place for me," Carter said.

"Pussy is pussy."

He waved his hand. "Nah, brother, it ain't. I have five sisters and my mother in my business. I'm the only son."

"Yea, I get it," he agreed. "Okay, give me another hour and we will hit a new Jazz spot."

Carter grinned. "Now that's what's up. I can hang til then."

***

"Welcome to the Cool Jazz Spot." Greg said as they pulled into the parking lot. It was located in a shopping center in Roswell.

"I got the cover." Carter said. "You took care of drinks at the last place."

"Cool." Greg agreed.

After the cover was paid, they strolled in and assessed their surroundings. Carter noticed a few couples dancing and some at the bar eating and drinking. The entertainment was a live band and the hostess seated them quickly.

Sweet Mary, Mother of Jesus!

She was with a friend.

Must be a girl's night out.

"What's wrong?" Greg asked and followed Carter's stare to see what had caught his attention.

"It's Terri." Carter blinked out of his shock and tightened his grip on the back of his chair to relieve some tension.

Greg nudged him. "Go talk to her before she catches you staring."

He agreed and approached the table.

She caught his attention and offered her hand. "What brings you here?"

He helped her to her feet. She hugged him.

Damn did she smell good!

He savored the moment and refrained from restricting her release of him. He wanted more and now was not the time.

"I want to introduce you to my friend, Charlene."

The sistah must have lost her mind.

The only person he wanted to meet was her divorce attorney and this woman didn't look like she knew anything about law.

"Nice to meet you, Charlene." He extended his hand.

"Ooh, Terri was right. You are good looking," she said.

An arrogant smile swept across his face. Terri thought he was handsome. He wondered what she would say if he told her that she was the love of his lifetime.

She scolded her friend. "Cut it out. I'm not good at this. Carter, Charlene is single. I thought I'd introduce the two of you to each other. The rest is none of my business."

Carter and Charlene laughed. He quickly assessed the woman in front of him. She was attractive, light skinned, tall, dark brown eyes, and short-cropped hair. He would play the game with her, but he was still not over Terri.

"Let's dance."

Carter took her by the hand and led Charlene to the dance floor. The music was upbeat and they rocked to the tunes. He felt oddly detached to her and looked away on occasion while they danced.

He caught a glimpse of Terri at the table. She played with her napkin and sipped her drink. When the band slowed the pace of the music, he motioned for them to return to the table.

"Thanks for the dance." Charlene returned to her seat. "Do you have a card? Maybe we could have dinner sometime."

He reached into his pocket to give Charlene a card, but he didn't have any. He was thankful for that. He glanced down at Terri who frowned at the suggestion.

She looked into his eyes and forced a smile. Her lips were pursed, and her eyebrows creased. She leaned back and folded her arms across her chest. "Good idea. The two of you should go out."

He reached down and tugged Terri's hand. "Come with me for a moment."

"Okay."

He respectfully led her into a slow dance. He carefully brought her close and swayed her in time with the music. His cheek pressed against hers. Her hand in his.

Her breasts were firmly locked against his chest. His hand placed in the small of her back. His lips were lost in the strands of her hair. He closed his eyes and imagined the two of them alone and not in the middle of a noisy nightclub.

She nestled her cheek against his neck. He took deep breaths to slow the fast pace of his heart. He stepped from side to side and she followed his steps effortlessly.

He savored the precious time he had with her only to lose her at the completion of the song.

"How have you been, Terri?" he asked in a deep, sultry, sexy voice.

Her body quaked, and her eyes immediately looked into his. He knew it was not the message but his delivery that startled her.

Still in his embrace, her lips quivered. "I-I'm well, Carter. Er, uh, are, uh, you okay?"

"Yea, Terri, I'm good," he answered. His eyes bored into hers. He released her when she leaned back.

"That's good, Carter. Wha-why don't you dance with Charlene again?" she stammered.

He shrugged. "Is that what you want?"

Her eyes were fixed into his stare. "No. Uh, I, um…"

She took several steps back from him, collided with another person that broke the trance between them. She made her apologies and darted to the table.

He stood there and cursed himself for blowing his cool on his feelings for her.

Greg came over. "You okay?"

"I'm good." Carter wiped his brow with the back of his hand. "Let's get out of here."

"Nah not yet. Don't let her know that she got to you. I got some wings for us. Let's eat."

CHAPTER 9

"Are you going to run for chapter president?"

Carter asked Greg in the middle of dinner at Noel's House of Jazz. They were joined by a fellow frat member, Trent Davenport.

"Naw, man, I've got too much work. A brother needs play time." Greg winked.

Carter laughed, lifted his hand and waved for the server to come to the table so they could order drinks. The thick sister with the black t-shirt stretched tightly against her breasts acknowledged them and walked over to the table.

"Scotch on the rocks." Trent said before Carter could get his order in.

Carter exclaimed. "Damn, brother. Where have you been traveling lately? I thought you were a gin drinker."

Trent and Greg laughed.

Carter lifted his head to the server. "Jack and Coke."

The server moved away and stood by Greg, "And for you, Sweetie?"

"Give me the Godfather on the rocks and put all the drinks on my tab." He beamed and flashed his platinum card. She accepted the card and walked away after she penciled in his order on her notepad.

"It's been a long time since we were able to hang out." Greg said and leaned back in his chair.

"My job is kicking my ass." Carter said and stared at Greg, "Why didn't you tell me it would be that rough?"

"Self-employment is rough. I need to advertise more inside and outside of our community." Trent said while he swayed his shoulders to the music that played in the background.

"Are we the only ones left that aren't married in the frat?" Greg asked.

Trent answered, "The only ones that are over thirty and under forty. The youngsters don't count. They shouldn't be married yet."

Carter spoke, "A lot of men marry in their twenties…"

"…and divorce by their thirties. I chose to skip all of that." Greg finished.

The server came by and set the drinks in front of the men.

Terri should be divorced.

She should have never married that fool.

"And he sure as hell doesn't deserve her."

He was startled by his outburst. He would've blamed it on the Jack, but he hadn't gotten a good taste of it yet.

Greg threw back a large mouthful of his drink and grabbed a few pretzels from the middle of the table. "Who the hell are you talking about?"

Carter cleared his throat. "Terri."

"Ah man." Greg threw up his hands. "Give it up."

"You know if he messes up, I'm making my move. There is no shame in my game. I should have made my move before he did. Now the brother doesn't appreciate what he has."

Trent dismissed his statement. "Ricky's wife? She wouldn't roll out with you. I met her. She's not your type. Talking that bullshit."

Carter's eyes narrowed and he clenched his fingers together underneath the table. "Let Ricky walk and we'll see what happens. If I get my shot at Terri again, she won't be out of my sight either. I heard Doug was possessive. I'd make him look like he's just playing."

"This is nonsense." Greg grinned and leaned back in his chair. "I'm with Trent. Married women are trouble, especially if her man catches you."

***

Carter read on a flyer that Noel's House of Jazz was looking for new talent to play music in the evenings. He left his friends at the table to find the owner. He wandered over to the bar and caught the attention of the bartender with short-cropped hair.

"Excuse me. Where do I find Noel?"

"She's here. I'll get one of the waitresses to bring her to you."

Carter leaned against the bar and watched the couples and singles mingle and listen to the soft jazz selection.

A couple he noticed in particular must have been on a date. She had her dark hair pressed and her long slender arms held the martini glass ever so delicately. Her mauve lipstick parted showing her pearly whites. She laughed at the remarks from her date and waved her glass. She was a beautiful woman but no Terri…

"May I help you?"

His trance broken, Carter turned to smile at the mature African-American woman who he assumed was Noel.

She had a friendly face and deep brown eyes. Her Angela Davis afro, the short version, was a blend of black and grey. She reminded him of his Aunt Sadie when she smiled because she had a small gap between her front teeth.

He liked her instantly. He offered her his hand, which she quickly brushed away.

"I give hugs."

He placed his cheek against hers and wrapped her in a light embrace.

"What can I do for you, nephew?" she grinned.

For some reason, she made him miss his mother. "I'd like a part-time job playing the piano for you. I'm not in a group but I play well."

"What's your name, son?"

"Carter Patrick Glass." He was slightly nervous. He clasped his hands behind his back.

She placed her fingers on the pearls she had around her neck. "I have an opening on Wednesday evenings, but you'll have to audition for me. Can you be here early next Wednesday so I can see your talents?"

"Yes, ma'am, I'll be here."

***

"I'm auditioning tonight for Noel's House of Jazz. Do you want to come?" Carter asked Ricky over the phone. His audition was in a couple of hours and he wanted support from a few of his friends.

"Man, not tonight. I've got plans." Ricky answered.

Carter heard shuffling and then her voice echoed through the phone.

"Hi."

He swallowed hard and hoped to get past the lump that suddenly formed in his throat.

"Hi," he paused.

Now what?

I've never had a problem talking to her before.

See if she'll come. Let his ass go out without her.

"I was telling Ricky that I have an audition this evening. Can you come?"

"Sure, I'll come. I'll see if someone can come with me."

You'll come?

"Ahem." He coughed slightly and finished the conversation. "I'll see you tonight. Noel's House of Jazz. Eight o'clock."

***

He arrived at Noel's on time to play. The parking lot was full, and the place was crowded. When he came in the door, he spotted Noel right away. She was dressed in a white sequin gown with thin shoulder straps and a tight bodice that enhanced her full figure. She was lovely and greeted him as he came closer to her.

"Hello, nephew. Are you ready to play?"

"I am, Miss Noel."

"I'm taking my chances tonight. My regular pianist moved away and I'm desperate for entertainment. I sell more drinks when I've got an act going on."

He kissed her on the cheek. "You won't be disappointed."

He took a seat at the piano. He stretched his arms and fingers before placing them on the keys. The volume in the room quieted down and all he heard was his keystrokes. His Jazz selection started off-key because he struck a few chords incorrectly due to his adjustment to the unfamiliar piano. In the middle of the song, he relaxed. He received a round of applause at the end of the selection.

Noel stood by the piano while he played. She lavished in her newfound talent. "A little rough at the beginning, but let's hear some more."

He assessed the crowded room and there she was.

Terri took a seat at a table near the piano.

Their eyes met.

He bit the inside of his cheek so he wouldn't go into a full-blown smile.

She was here to see him and that was all that mattered.

This one's for you. He mouthed the words through his lips.

She cheerfully waved.

He focused on the keys, took a deep breath, and exhaled to get himself in the proper mindset. He pulled the mic toward him. Noel winced as if she wasn't expecting him to sing.

He sang Larry Graham's "One in a Million You" with every emotion he could find in his heart over the keys.

There wasn't a sound in the place other than his voice and music he played on the piano.

Once the song was completed, he had a standing ovation. He glanced up at Noel.

She grinned, "Now that's what I'm talking about, nephew. You got it if you want it."

Carter shook her hand and hugged her. He peered over her shoulder and saw Terri standing and clapping at his finished piece.

Noel's eyes lowered, and she placed her hand on his shoulder. "She's the one, isn't she?"

"Yeah." He paused before adding the rest. "She's married."

Noel squeezed his shoulder. "And you're in love with her. Ain't life grand? She's waiting for you. Go talk to her."

"Thank you, ma'am."

He walked towards Terri and she pushed her chair aside to get to him. She wrapped her arms around his waist and hugged him. He lifted his arms and wrapped her in a light hug. He couldn't stand not being able to hold her beyond a friendly way.

"How did you like song?" he asked.

She released her hold of his waist. "You mean the panty throwing voice?" She teased. "If you weren't a friend and I wasn't married…"

"Don't go there," he laughed. "I have to get back to my set."

CHAPTER 10

He opened his silverware drawer, lifted the tray, and put it on the counter. Hidden underneath was a picture of Terri in her wedding dress. He was over Terri's house when the photos came back from the photographer. He was offered a few of the pictures and this one in particular made its way home amongst the other pictures that were gifted to him.

Damn she looked amazing.

He sighed, placed the picture back in the drawer and then put the silverware tray back on top.

Why torture myself?

What's done was done.

She'd made her decision. Time to move on.

The ringing phone interrupted his thoughts.

He went to the living room to retrieve it.

"Hello." He breathed the words through the receiver and hoped that his voice would wrap around her heart.

"It's me reminding you about my sister's wedding rehearsal tomorrow night. You don't have to be there, but you said you wanted to come. Are you still planning on it?"

"I'll be there for you, eh, them. I'll be there for them."

"Great. I'll see tomorrow. Bye."

"Bye."

She hung up.

"I love you, Terri."

***

"Thanks for coming to the rehearsal dinner. I'm sorry I put you to work today. It was supposed to be a relaxed event." Lisa said to Carter.

He chuckled, "No problem. I have enough wedding experience to know that it's stressful."

A woman with long micro braids walked up to the pair. "Hi, I'm Stacy. I remember you from Terri's wedding."

"Carter," he smiled.

"I'll let you guys talk." Lisa said. "I know Doug is looking for me and if he isn't, he will be soon. Take care."

"We didn't talk much at Terri's wedding. I teach piano on the side and do collections for a living."

"Impressive. I play at Noel's House of Jazz on Wednesday's as well as referee basketball. I work at Parker Logistics as a purchasing manager."

"Did you eat yet?" she motioned towards the buffet table.

"Not yet."

"Grab a plate and come sit with me. We'll chat about music and stuff."

"Sure."

He followed her through to the buffet table where several guests had already served themselves. He and Stacy located an empty table. They chatted for about fifteen minutes when his plate moved from under him. He looked up and it was Terri.

"I see you've met my cousin." She held his plate in her hand. Her face was stoic and unfriendly.

What was going on?

"I'll get this for you and I'll bring you a slice of pound cake. I made it early this morning."

She left.

Stacy snickered.

"What?" he asked.

"Oh, nothing." She stood up and took her empty plate to the table reserved for dirty dishes and returned with one slice of pound cake. "Terri will bring yours and... here she comes."

Terri sat beside Carter.

"Where's Ricky?" Stacy said in a teasing voice.

"Not here." Terri said coldly and looked at Carter. "How's the pound cake?"

He picked up his fork and took a bite. "Delicious." He wasn't sure what to make of the interaction between the women.

"Good." Terri said and scooted closer to him.

Greg walked up to the table. "Dog, you got a minute?"

He looked at both women and answered "Sure. Excuse me ladies."

He followed Greg.

"Let's get some air."

The men walked outside and were a few feet away from Dupree Country Club.

"What's up?" Carter asked.

"Did you see what went on? I don't think Terri liked you talking to her cousin. I thought I'd save you from getting your ass kicked."

He smiled and nodded, "Really?"

Terri was jealous?

"Just be cool about it. I know how you feel about her. If you're going to move on, stay out of her family. You don't want the shit to get messy."

"Thanks for the heads up."

"No problem."

***

On Doug and Lisa's wedding day, he was up and ready for his gig as the keyboard player for the happy couple. He arrived at Dupree Country Club dressed in a light grey suit.

He hadn't seen Terri yet. He knew she would arrive soon.

He sat behind the piano and played a few selections for the arriving guests.

On cue, he played the requested music for the entrance of the mothers. Shortly, thereafter, the bridesmaids took deliberate strides down the aisle. He glanced up and saw Terri. He almost missed his notes and forced himself to remain focused.

After the ceremony, Carter stayed for the reception. He was able to get a good view of her from a distance. She looked extraordinary in her light rose gown.

She caught his attention and made her way towards him.

"Thank you for being here, Carter."

She hugged him.

He refrained from allowing his emotions to follow. He purposely peered off into the distance, savored the moment and yet trembled with fear. His feelings for her were too obvious to hide.

He secretly wished that they were standing alone on a tropical island. No Ricky, no friends, no family and no marriage. Rewind back to when they met. His choices would have been different.

"You're welcome."

"You look great in your suit." She fingered his lapel. She was close enough to for him to get a whiff of her perfume and her lips were within inches from his.

"Thanks. Lisa and Doug look really happy." His brown eyes blazed into hers.

"They are," she agreed.

"How are you doing? I'm here if you need me." He lifted his head and noticed Ricky holding a drink.

The brother frowned at Carter and Terri.

She tilted her head in the direction of her husband and quickly removed her hand from Carter's lapel.

She nervously responded. "Thank you. I have to go. I think Lisa needs me." She glanced over at Ricky before she walked away.

Damn.

Caught doing something that I wasn't doing.

She made the first move.

If it's true that she wants me to stay single, when will she get rid of her husband?

***

He noticed his friend, Maya, was sitting alone. He wandered over to talk to her.

"Are you enjoying the wedding?"

Maya shuddered before she spoke. She was startled by the sound of his voice. "Um, yeah, sure."

"You don't sound very happy." He said and took the empty seat next to her.

"I am," she sighed.

He leaned his shoulder toward hers. "I told you that pink was a good color for you."

Maya laughed. "You're just being polite but thanks anyway."

"Did you bring someone special?"

She shook her head and dismissed him. "Come on. The guy I like will never notice me, besides, I'm sure he's seeing someone else. Has that ever happened to you?"

He responded. "Yes, it has."

"I'm going home now. I'm tired of watching him ignore me." She stood up to leave and he stood with her. "Thanks for listening to me. You have been so kind to me and a good friend." She hugged him.

"I'll walk you to your car."

"Thanks," she said. "I'm sure I'll be fine."

"No problem. I could use some fresh air."

***

After he returned from walking Maya to her car, he entered the hall and heard Ricky and Terri's voices. He moved back into the doorway so he could hear the conversation without being noticed.

"Where in the hell have you been?" Ricky demanded.

"I stayed at my sister's house. I wasn't in the mood to fight with you." Terri sneered.

"You still should have let me know your whereabouts."

"Why did you bring that fool Chris to my sister's wedding? He was not an invited guest."

Ricky became loud and hateful. "Well I invited him to come with me. What's up with Doug and his gay ass guests?"

"Keep your voice down. If it was whom I think you are talking about, Dr. Zwinger is a world-renowned counselor. He brought his partner. Those men were invited. Your friend Chris wasn't."

"I don't see a lot of black men here. Your family is whacked. They are running around like slaves tending to the white man just happy that their daughter found a rich one."

"I am tired of arguing with you on this. Ever since we got married, you have been mean and hateful."

"I'm sick of this argument. I'm sorry I came home."

Carter had heard enough. He approached the couple and the argument stopped.

Ricky glanced at Carter and then back to Terri. "We'll talk later."

"Hey Frat, y'all okay?" Carter extended his hand.

Ricky reciprocated with the secret handshake. "It's all good."

Ricky looked past Carter's shoulder. Chris was at the end of the hall and beckoned him to come.

"Excuse me, frat." Ricky frowned at Terri. "I'm going to let your *boy* talk to you."

He glared at Carter before he left to see Chris.

Terri's eyes were glossed over with tears. She was angry, and Carter couldn't make it better.

"Sorry. I hope no one heard us." She opened her clutch bag, pulled out a napkin, and dabbed her eyes.

He lowered his face and his lips grazed her ear. He softly whispered, "I'm here whenever you need me."

"Thank you," she sniffled and turned her shoulder away from him. "Lisa needs me."

She brushed past him and disappeared amongst the guests.

***

"Miss Mona, how are you?" he asked and wrapped the elder woman in a light hug.

She reciprocated his embrace. "I'm well and enjoying the party."

"I bet you're excited about the baby."

"I am." She beamed with pride. "My sister is in spirit, so I've taken the grandma role for her grandchildren."

His focus wasn't on their conversation. He gazed across the reception hall to see if Terri was still at the wedding.

"I think everyone knows that you're in love with her." Startled by the interruption, his eyes held a flash of shock. He'd forgotten Mona was still standing next to him.

"What are you talking about?"

She lifted her face to his and captured his full attention. "You wanted to marry her. You wanted to stop her wedding. You haven't taken your eyes off her."

He was speechless.

How much did Mona know?

"Who are you talking about?"

He didn't understand how women like Noel and Mona were able to see his love for Terri.

His heart sank and involuntarily, he sighed. "Please don't tell her or her husband. She must never know about this."

"I won't." Mona said softly.

"How did you know?" He didn't realize his devotion to Terri was that obvious.

"I saw the look in your eyes when you talked to her. You look at her the same way that Doug looks at Lisa."

Carter stood there emotionally stunned. The more time passed, the more his resistance weakened at Terri's presence. He was in love with her and it was becoming harder to deny the truth.

She said sternly, "Wait for her to come to you. Expect the unexpected. She will need you."

He sighed. He wasn't sure how to take Mona's advice. From what he'd seen from Terri, he knew the marriage was strained and probably wouldn't last long.

And no matter how much he wanted it to end, he didn't want the woman he loved hurt in the process.

CHAPTER 11

Carter spent his Wednesday nights pouring out his sorrow for the love that he'd lost over the keyboard at Noel's House of Jazz.

Once a week was enough to release his tension and keep his fingers in shape for his musically talented hands.

Sometimes his selections were somber and sometimes they were cheery and soulful.

Occasionally he took requests.

Tonight, he faced his past.

There Terri sat, alone with her glass of white wine. He tried not to allow her presence to be a distraction. When it was time for break, he approached Terri. Sadness and distress were in her deep brown oval eyes. Her dark hair was pulled up and her face was puffy as if she'd been crying

He took an empty chair next to her. "I didn't know you were coming. Thanks for being here."

"I had to get away for a while. I didn't know where else to go," she said sadly.

"Is everything okay?"

"No, it's not. Some white woman keeps calling me and hanging up the phone. I have her number. I asked Ricky about it and he got upset. I don't know what to do."

As his mother always said, the chickens would come home to roost.

He now understood what that expression meant.

Ricky was still playing around.

Carter didn't want to be in the middle of their domestic dispute, but he couldn't leave Terri. Because even though he hated seeing her hurting, the spark in him that held out hope was delighted that maybe, just maybe, this meant he might have a chance to win her after all.

He scooted his chair closer to hers, placed his hand confidently, comfortingly on her knee. Held her gaze. Tried to play the part of good friend consoling someone in need, offering the faint hope they both knew wasn't real but was expected between them. "I'm sure Ricky has an explanation. Probably some old girlfriend is trying to start trouble. Don't worry about it. I'm here if you need me."

"There's more. I've found lipstick on his clothes, some woman's earring; he's working weird hours and, sometimes, when I call him, he rushes me off the phone."

"What's his explanation?"

"The lipstick…he said that he went to see his mother and she kissed him. The earring belonged to some client that rode in his car. Sometimes I can't reach him at all and his explanation is that his battery died on his phone and he forgot to charge it. This isn't right. Something's going on."

"My heart hurts for you. I don't like to see you in despair." He lightly stroked her back, grabbed a clean linen napkin from the table, and offered it to her.

Finally!

The heavens opened and answered his prayers. The heaviness in his heart was lifted. This was the beginning of the end of a marriage to a man who didn't deserve her. His happiness with her was eminent.

"I shouldn't have told you this. You and Ricky are friends." She sniffled and sipped her drink. She brushed the hair back from her face.

He lifted her hand and caressed his thumb on the back of her palm. "You and I are friends too. My door is always open if you need me. I have to finish my set. Will you be here afterwards?"

"No," she squeezed his hand. "I have to go home and settle this. Thanks for listening and being a good friend. I'll see you soon. I still owe you dinner."

He smirked. "I'll hold you to that."

He stood up to leave and finished his set. As his music, wound down and he readied himself to leave, Noel motioned for him to sit with her.

"Hello, Miss Noel."

"Hello, nephew. Was that her that was here tonight?"

"Yes, ma'am."

"I hope you have that situation under control. I don't want any jealous husbands shooting up my place."

Carter laughed. "No, ma'am. You witnessed it. I only spent five minutes with her."

"But if the opportunity arose, you would spend more time with her," Noel stated.

"Yes, ma'am."

"Creeping with a married woman in a troubled relationship can be dangerous."

"How did you know she was troubled?" Carter asked.

"She came here twice without her man. There's a reason for that. She needs you and she knows that she can't have you."

He sat back for a moment and thought about Noel's strong words. He hugged her and thanked her for her motherly advice. He stepped briskly to his car, drove off and wondered what he should do next.

Terri needed more information. Something that would be the ultimate deal breaker.

"That's it!" he shouted from behind the wheel. "I'll get a private detective to follow him."

He arrived home, parked his car in the garage and hoped that, decision made, answers obtained, Terri would finally see the truth of her husband, and that it was Carter who she could count on.

CHAPTER 12

It was a long morning at church with his sister Joy. He pulled into his driveway, entered his home, and sat his keys on the kitchen table. He was glad to be home to unwind.

The Braves game was on and he was ready to watch it. He pulled a brew out of the fridge, sat down on the couch with his feet on the ottoman, and dozed. The doorbell rang and shortened his nap.

He opened it and there she was on his doorstep.

Didn't he just get the lecture on lust and coveting thy neighbor's wife?

God was testing him in many ways.

He got the lesson this morning and the temptation this afternoon.

God must be laughing his butt off.

"Hi. I'm only staying a minute." Terri said.

A minute was all he needed to take in his Nubian queen. She was there unannounced and brought a dish of food. He stepped aside and allowed her to enter. He peeked outside to see if Ricky was with her and there was no one else.

"What's up?"

"I promised you dinner and I brought it by. I can't eat it with you. I'm going to my mother's house."

She set the dish on the counter and he walked over to see what she brought. He uncovered the foil and lifted the dinner to his nose. The faint sweet smell of cheese sent sensations of hunger pangs in through his nose and down to his stomach. Whatever she brought, he was eating it.

"It's chicken lasagna. I hope you enjoy it."

"I will. Thanks."

"It's cold."

"I'll go heat it up." He went to the kitchen and beckoned her to follow. He took the lasagna and heated it up in the stove.

"I didn't interrupt anything did I?"

"I was watching the game. Can you stay a few?"

She glanced at her watch. "Only for a few. My parents are expecting me."

They went back into the living room. He sat on the recliner and Terri sat on the end of the couch next to him. He was unsure of what conversation to have with her. He wanted her to relax and stay as long as she could, but he knew that this was no place for a wedded woman.

"How's Ricky?" The words came out of his mouth, but he didn't care. He asked to get the unpleasantness out of the way.

"He's fine, I think. I don't know. He's been mean and strange lately."

His eyebrows creased. "How so?"

"I don't know. What about you? How are you?"

"I could be better."

"You're going to have to get over her." She folded her legs under her on the couch. She grabbed the blanket from the other end.

"Who?" He picked up the remote and lowered the volume on the TV.

"Cynthia."

He gazed into her eyes, blinked, and didn't say a word.

"I think that's why you won't let me fix you up with my friends. It must be tough for you. I didn't like her, but you and Cynthia were together a long time. You never told me what happened?"

He shrugged. "It didn't work so we parted. It was for the best."

She accepted his answer and relaxed on the couch. Suddenly, she sat up with a puzzled look.

He watched her expression and questioned her. "What's wrong?"

"I think my lasagna is burning."

He jumped up from the couch and ran to the kitchen. The smoke alarm sounded just as he arrived.

Smoke came from the stove. He quickly turned it off, grabbed a towel, and waved the fumes away from the alarm. She opened the kitchen window and patio door to let in some air. He cautiously pulled the crispy dinner out of the stove.

She laughed at her burned lasagna. "Remind me never to have you warm up dinner for me."

He was not amused. "I'm sorry. You made dinner for me and I lost track of time."

"That's okay. I'll make it again for you. Next time I'll heat it up first."

"Thanks."

Terri weakly smiled at him, went into the living room, and grabbed her purse. He followed her and walked her to the door.

"I'm sorry. I have to go now. I'll see you soon."

CHAPTER 13

He arrived solo to the Valentine's Dance hosted by his fraternity. He hadn't asked anyone to the dance and promised to assist with the bartending if needed.

Terri and Ricky arrived while he was at the bar ordering a drink and conversing with Doug.

His gaze moved unerringly to her. Doug nudged him. "Did you get what you want?"

"No," he breathed. "I didn't."

Doug's head turned and followed Carter's stare.

"Maybe next time." Doug clasped his shoulder. "I'm heading back to the table."

"I'm coming." Carter took a swig of his Jack and Coke.

She wore a long white gown with a fade of red that started from the knees. As he approached the table, he noticed that she barely had time to sit down before Ricky grabbed her hand and took her to the dance floor.

Carter settled in his chair and watched the pair. Terri's body was pressed against Ricky's but she barely looked at him. She had a tight smile on her face. When Ricky lowered his lips to her ear, she pursed her lips and frowned. The couple didn't dance long and walked back to the table.

Lisa stood from her chair, which broke his attention to Terri. She pulled Terri's hand before she could sit down. "I need to fix my makeup. Come with me."

"Yes," Terri huffed. "I need some fresh air."

***

One of the bartenders had to leave early, so Carter took his place behind the bar rather than in front of it. He was drying a wine glass when Terri sat down in front of him. "What can I get you, pretty lady?"

Terri rested her elbow on the bar and smiled. "Appletini, please."

"My pleasure."

Carter dropped the ingredients in a mixer, shook it briskly and poured her drink in a martini glass. He placed the napkin down, slid the drink in front of her and topped it with a cherry. He stepped back, and she raised her hand to halt him from leaving her.

"How are you?"

His eyes bored into hers. "I'm well, and you?"

"I'm fine," she picked up her napkin and placed it on her lap.

"I'm here if you need me."

She blinked to break the connection. "Okay. I'll keep that in mind. Can I ask you something?

He cocked his head and rested his palms on the bar. "Sure."

"Why didn't you bring a date?"

His lips parted, and jaw lowered as he searched for words to answer her. Nothing came to mind.

She stroked the stem of her glass with her fingertips. "I think you're still in love with Cynthia. Have you seen her lately?"

"No. I haven't," he said in a noncommittal voice.

"You should call her. I'm sure she'd like to hear from you."

He knew that Cynthia would never see him again. He was in love with another woman and she was sitting right in front of him.

"You've mentioned her before. Are you really interested in Cynthia and me getting back together?"

She gasped.

Her lips parted, and she held her glass mid-stream. He walked over to her and lowered his face within inches of hers. She put her glass down and leaned in slightly.

"Not really," she slowly admitted and stared directly into his eyes. She closed her lips and slowly leaned back. He mirrored her move and straightened his back to a standing position.

"How's your cousin, Stacy?"

She pursed her lips and frowned. "She's fine."

He lowered his face close to hers. His lips were close enough to almost taste her lipstick. "How long are we going to continue to play this game?"

"Bartender."

He leaned back and acknowledged the patron. "Give me a minute, please."

"Well, that was awkward." She tittered and broke the building tension. She picked up her glass and downed her martini. "I could use another one."

He lowered his eyes to her glass. "You sure?"

"Absolutely. I have to deal with that asshole husband of mine and this will help."

"Let me get him first, and then I'll make you another one." He slung a towel over his shoulder and walked away.

***

"Can you take this trash out in the back?"

"Sure," Carter replied. "I'll be back in a minute."

He went through the kitchen to the back doors. A couple of cooks were snickering, and the back door was partially open.

"What's up?" Carter asked with the bag of trash in his hand."

The cook with the blue apron answered. "You don't want to go out there."

"Why not?"

"Some couple is getting their freak on. He must have hit her G-spot. You can hear her over the dishwasher."

The tall cook with the long black beard doubled over laughing. "I want a piece of that action."

"Fellas, I'll be back. If she came then they're probably gone. This won't take but a minute."

Carter exited through the doors and walked neared the dumpster.

"Uh, Uh, Uh…" the sound was louder with every step he took.

"Oh, Ricky!" she wailed.

Carter paused in his tracks.

"Keep your damn voice down."

Carter recognized the man. There was no mistake that it belonged to Ricky Burke. Carter's chest tightened. Although he wasn't able to see the pair, he knew that they were close. He threw the trash into the dumpster and it landed with a loud thud.

"Blah, cough."

"God dammit! Your drunk ass threw up over my thousand-dollar suit," yelled Ricky. I've got to clean this up."

Carter turned his back and stormed back into the kitchen.

The tall cook stopped him. "Well?"

Carter was still stunned at what he just heard. He pressed his lips tight and answered. "They're done."

He had no idea what to do with this information. Ricky was having a freak getting drunk over his dumb ass.

It was none of his business, but it was definitely his business. Terri needed to divorce Ricky. The sooner the better.

Carter approached the bar still reeling from what he'd seen.

A patron caught his attention to serve a drink. He washed his hands and threw a towel over his shoulder. He glanced down the bar and watched Terri. Her hands were on the stem of the glass and her eyes were cast down in wishful thought.

That was the third martini that I served her.

I'm glad she's not driving or I would've cut her off.

That man is causing nothing but grief and misery. The alcohol won't make it better.

Greg sat down next to Terri. "You okay."

Carter approached the pair to ease in on the conversation.

"I'm fine," she sighed. "I haven't been able to find Ricky for the last thirty minutes."

"My date disappeared too." Greg said wistfully. "We've been having issues. I thought we'd have a good time tonight, but I haven't seen her in a while."

"The Godfather?" Carter offered.

"Nah," Greg waived him away. "I've had two too many already. Better not."

Ricky walked into the room wiping his suit.

Carter's eyes narrowed, jaw tightened, and his lips were pressed tight.

Ricky ignored him and approached Terri. "Are you finished talking to your boy?"

She eyed her husband. "He's busy being a host. Where have you been and what's that smell?"

"Somebody that couldn't hold their liquor threw up on me. I need to change so we've got to go."

"I want to stay awhile."

"I said let's go unless you want to stay here and have your *boy* take you home." Ricky yelled.

Carter pressed his lips tight and turned his head. He listened to make sure Terri was okay. Another guest captured his attention to order a drink.

"I know you want to sleep with him." Ricky's loud voice was heard across the bar.

Carter snapped his head around and looked at the pair. He couldn't believe what he heard. He walked over to the couple and gave Ricky a deadpan stare.

"You're changing the subject. Don't bring Carter into this. You never answered my question. Where the hell have you been?"

"I said let's go," he grabbed her hand and dragged her off the chair. She stumbled, stood and faced her husband.

Carter moved to come around the bar and Greg put his hand in front of Carter's face and caught his eye.

"Marital business."

"Fine," she said and pushed her empty martini glass away from her. "We're leaving. We can finish this at home."

Terri marched away from the bar. Ricky followed.

Carter's anger tightened in his chest. He picked up her empty glass and twirled it in his hand.

The results were in from the Fellows' Detective agency. Hell, he'd heard the truth himself, even if he didn't have visual proof.

Now he had to decide on how and when she would receive them.

CHAPTER 14

"Carter speaking."

"It's Terri. Do you have time to meet me for coffee this morning?"

"Sure."

"Starbucks, Roswell, 9:00 a.m."

It had been a couple of months since the Valentine's Day event. He thought of her often and hoped that she was okay.

He hadn't seen her and was surprised by her call.

He pulled into the parking lot and she was waiting inside. He leaned in to kiss her on the cheek, but she tilted her head away. He leaned back to his standing position. "Do you want me to get you anything?"

"I'm fine. Get your coffee and we'll chat."

He brought his coffee back to the table and sat across from her. Since she didn't welcome his affection, he sensed that a serious talk was coming.

"How've you been?" he asked and leaned back in his chair. His eyes glistened with sadness and his heart ached for her.

"I'm fine," she said pensively. "I've got a lot going on. I'm holding off on starting the business until next year."

His eyes lit up with shock and he sat up straight in his chair. "Why? You love catering. It's your passion to cook."

"Timing and now is not it." She flicked a gaudy sea green scrunchie bracelet on her wrist.

"When did you get that?" Carter creased his eyebrows. "You hate scrunchies."

She waved her hand dismissively. "It's some peace offering gift from my husband."

"I would've never bought you that. You like real crystals and gemstones. As I recall lapis lazuli is your favorite." He resisted his urge to touch her and placed his free hand in his lap.

"It is." She smiled weakly. "You remembered."

He lowered his eyes to the bracelet. "How do you like it?"

"Meh," she shrugged.

She sipped her coffee and sighed. "I've been meaning to call you. About the Valentine's dance... Well... Thank you for coming to my rescue."

He shook his head. "No problem."

"I need to work things out with my husband."

His heart sank to the pit of his stomach.

"We're going to counseling."

He forced a smile through his lips and sank back in his chair. "That's great. I hope it works out for you."

"We'll see." She shrugged her shoulders. "How are you? All we seem to talk about are my issues."

He sat up straight and stared in her eyes. "I'm well. Still doing my part-time gigs and keeping the kids when Joy needs me."

"Ah yes," she smiled and sipped her coffee. "Shante and Kinte. I never did teach her how to cook. I'm sure she's upset with me."

"She'll be fine. She's torturing her brother. That will keep her busy for a while."

Terri chuckled. "Carter," she said wistfully. "You've been a really good friend. I miss our talks."

He nodded. "I've stayed away so you can handle your business. I don't like to see you hurt."

"I know…" she softly replied. " I love him and I married him. It has to get better."

It broke him, to hear her say the words he'd most wanted her to deny.

It was time to let her go.

She reached for his hand and he pulled away, rose to stand. "Take care of yourself. Terri. I've got to get to a meeting, but," he paused, unable to stop himself from offering even as her words cut him to shreds, "I'll always be here if you need me."

She looked up at him, her eyes welling with tears. "Thanks. We'll see each other again soon."

"Goodbye."

***

Noel's House of Jazz was crowded. Instead of his usual piano selection, Noel had a guest band and Carter was acting as the keyboardist for the group.

Across the room, he recognized Doug and Lisa. Although it was dark, the man's sandy blonde hair and the light reflection on his glasses called Carter's attention to the couple.

Once his group took a break, he walked over to sit with them.

"My man," he extended his hand to Doug, who stood up to complete his greeting with a firm grip.

"Good to see you," Doug smiled.

Lisa remained seated and waved from her chair.

Carter extended his hand to shake hers and looked at her swollen abdomen. "You haven't had that baby yet?"

"No," she sighed. "My husband thinks that Noel's spicy wings will get this baby moving. I'm due any day now."

Carter laughed and knelt down between the pair. "The wings are spicy. I won't touch those. It would take a week for me to recover."

They laughed.

He turned to Doug. "You've got her out late."

"Yes," he chuckled. "I do. The family party is tomorrow at her sister's house. We'll stay for a little while longer. This may be the last day before we're a family of three."

Carter turned to Lisa. "How's Terri?"

Lisa hesitated, looked at her husband then back at Carter. "I think you should call her."

He was startled by her response. "Why? Is she okay?"

"She's could use a friend."

Carter whipped his head around to look at Doug.

The man's face was grim as he took a swig of his vodka.

What the hell was going on?

"Just think about it." Lisa interjected. "Ooh, this baby is shaking my stomach. I hope he will let me eat."

Carter stood up and looked down at the pair. "I have to return to my set. If you're here afterwards, I'll stop by and we can talk more. It was good to see the both of you."

They waved as he walked away.

Terri had just about told him to stay out of her affairs, but from what he'd just heard, the counseling must not to be going well.

Maybe, just maybe, they would still have their chance to be together.

CHAPTER 15

"Dog," Greg exclaimed over the phone. "You missed the frat meeting."

"Joy's kids. I couldn't bring them. From the sound of your voice, I must have missed some good shit."

"You did. Ricky's wife moved out."

"Say what!" Carter couldn't believe what he heard. He gripped the phone tightly and pressed it to his ear. He wondered if he heard the message correctly. "Terri moved out."

"She did. The rumor is that she got tired of his shit. She cleaned out the bank account, cashed in the liquid investments, and moved into her own place."

"Damn!" God had listened to his prayers. He commenced his personal celebration. About damn time. He was freaking happy that she was no longer putting up with Ricky's drama. The heaviness in his heart was lifted and he felt like he was flying through the air.

"Brotha is pissed. She moved while he was out of town. Only her family knows where she lives."

No wonder Lisa and Doug told him to call her.

Terri left her husband and was in need of someone to talk to.

Ricky dug his grave and Carter didn't have to pass the shovel.

He was free to make his move.

"That's too bad." Carter popped his fist against his chest in celebration.

"Nah, brotha. It's not. You were ready to kick his ass Valentine's Day and I had to stop you. I can hear the celebration over here. Give her a call. I'm sure she'll want to talk to you."

"Nah," he said but couldn't stop grinning. "She specifically told me to stay out of her affairs and I need to respect that."

"Player, who are you fooling? You're dialing the digits as soon as I hang up."

Carter chuckled at Greg's comment. "Maybe."

"I'm hanging out with Omar and Carl. They are taking me out. I'll be the creepy old man at the club. The spots they hang out at, the women are a little younger."

"You better get ID before you talk to any of them then," Carter warned. "Your executive pay won't get you out of jail bait."

Greg laughed. "Yea, dog. I'm staying clean. Goodnight."

"Goodnight."

***

He had no plans.

It was Saturday evening and raining. He looked out of the window and watched the rain trickle down the glass. It was as if the earth was crying a flood of tears that he imagined that Terri was shedding.

He was really happy that Terri left Ricky, but wondered would she ever renew his and her friendship.

Although she left Ricky, she'd said that she was in love with him. It would take her time to forget about her ex.

A car with its headlights on pulled into his driveway.

He wasn't expecting company.

He moved to the door and his heart started racing when she got out of the car.

She walked quickly across the sidewalk up the steps.

He sucked in his cheeks so the inward smile wouldn't spread across his face.

He lowered his eyes and breathed a light sigh. "It's good to see you."

She folded her umbrella quickly, brushed past him, and lifted her eyes to his. "It's good to see you too. Is this a good time?"

"I'll always have time for you," he responded.

She lowered her eyes, sighed and looked up at him. "I owe you an apology. I was rude the last time we spoke at the coffee shop. The marital stress was getting to me and I shouldn't have taken it out on you."

He shook his head and his lips parted. He couldn't believe she was standing in his foyer and barely heard her apology. "Understandable."

She lowered her eyes and pulled out a casserole dish from her bag. "I brought chicken lasagna for you. You didn't get to eat it last time. I'll heat it up this time for you."

A smile broadened across his face. "And you'll get to stay longer this time?"

She grinned. "Yes, and I'll have a bite with you if you don't have plans."

He lightly wrapped his arms around her. "I plan to spend time with you." He kissed her on the forehead.

***

"For you," she placed a slice of lasagna in front of him. She sat in the chair cattycorner from his.

"Thank you and I appreciate you thinking of me." He placed his hand over hers in a firm squeeze.

"It was the least I could do," she said somberly and sectioned a piece of lasagna on her fork. She stared at the morsel, twirled it in the air, and then put it back on the plate.

"You sound down. Is there anything that I can do for you?"

"I left Ricky."

His jaw dropped.

Although he'd gotten the news from Greg, it was if he heard it for the first time.

"I'm not going back." She choked through unexpected tears.

"What the hell happened? Are you okay?" He exclaimed.

"Yes, I'm a big girl, I can handle my business." She sniffled and dabbed her face with her napkin. "I moved out two weeks ago and I haven't seen him since."

Two weeks ago?

"Why didn't you call me?"

"Because I needed to handle this. I have so many decisions to make." She wiped her cheek with the back of her hand.

"Take mine." He offered her his clean napkin. "At least tell me what happened. I need to know that you're okay."

"Well, I came home late Sunday morning after my nephew was born. I was really excited and ran up the stairs to tell Ricky about him. I heard the shower and looked at my home computer. It surprised me that it was on. I looked at it and Ricky's personal e-mail account was open. I searched for suspicious emails and found a candidate.

"The letter was from someone named Diane professing her love for Ricky. He returned the affection in the email. I was stunned by what I saw. I didn't know what to say. He appeared in the room as I was printing off the love letter. I took it, threw it at him, and marched away to the bedroom. The argument started there."

She sniffled and took a bite of her lasagna. She chewed it slowly.

"I knew he was going on a business trip. I packed my clothes and left while he was gone. We haven't spoken about his affair or anything else since."

"Where are you staying?"

"With my Aunt Lucille. She's out of town for the next month or so. I'm housesitting for her until I can figure this out."

"I'm sorry he did this to you." He covered her hand with his in a gentle caress. His Beauty needed him, and he was going to be there for her.

"I shouldn't be here, I need to leave." She looked up at him with tears stained in her cheeks. She pushed her chair back and rose from the table. Carter embraced her in his arms and she rested her head on his chest and hugged him tight.

He kissed her hair and whispered in her ear. "You're upset. You can't leave. Why don't you rest on the couch in the living room? You need your friends around you right now." He caressed her check and wiped away a couple of tears.

"It's been very difficult," she sighed.

He walked her to the couch, fluffed a few pillows and motioned for her to sit. He left the room and returned with a plaid blanked to cover her. She exhaled a loud sigh, closed her eyes and curled up under the blanket.

***

Carter believed he was free to make his move. He was careful not to allow his feelings for her to show and bold enough to call her often.

She was the one that his heart ached for. He stopped by her Aunt's house at least three times a week and called when he didn't come by.

He arrived for a visit late Friday evening and Terri's car was in the driveway.

"Come in," she said.

He crossed the threshold into her house.

"I'm just stopping by to see if you're okay."

"I know. You've been here all week. Thank you for coming. Good friends like you are hard to come by. Lisa and Brenda are worried about our friendship."

"Why?" he asked and put his hands in his pockets. He resisted the urge to wrap her in his arms.

"They think you're interested in me as more than a friend. I told them that you're just a really thoughtful guy. They're just a little overprotective."

"You're lucky to have family and friends that care about you. That includes me."

When she exhaled, her shoulders relaxed. "Thank you. I'm glad you're here. It's been tough. I can manage this. Don't worry about me."

He shifted his stance and moved toward the door. "I can't stay just in case your aunt comes home. I don't want her to get the wrong impression."

"She's still out of town. I'll let you know when she's back." She rubbed her eyes. "I'm really tired."

"I know." He perked up. "Let me take you to get some coffee."

"I don't know," she hesitated.

"I won't press you."

"Do you know what I'd like to have?"

"What's that?" he asked.

"Strawberry cheesecake from Elliot's Bakery."

"They're closed this late at night but there's a restaurant by my house that makes pretty good cheesecake. I can take you there if you want."

A smile swept across her weary face. "I'll get my purse."

After they purchased two slices of cheesecake, she agreed to go over to his place for a while. They settled in the kitchen.

Carter brewed coffee.

He knew that he must be careful with his time with her. She was still married, and she trusted him.

The aroma of the dark roast wafted through the air.

He brought the cups of coffee and sat beside her.

"How's the cheesecake?" he asked.

"Delicious." She savored her morsel and licked her tongue across her lips.

"Good." He forked a strawberry and ate it.

"Carter…"

"Yeah."

"Why do you think he did this to me?"

"I don't know. Just stupidity. What do you want to do about it?"

She slowly sipped her coffee, leaned back slightly, and briefly closed her eyes. She took in a deep breath and exhaled with exasperation.

"I don't know. I don't know what to do." She shook her head.

He reached under the table and took her hand. "I've always said that I'm here if you need me."

"I know, but..."

He squeezed her hand and pressed further. "I mean it. You should take some time to get away and think about this."

"I've got too much to do." She sighed and dismissed his statement.

He voice was filled with concern. "You've got to take care of yourself. Get out of Atlanta. Go with some friends. I'll go with you if you want."

She laughed. "Now Carter, where am I going with you?"

"Savannah."

The word jumped out of his mouth before he could retrieve them. He wanted Terri to himself and out of town seemed like the perfect solution. He hoped she didn't read too much into his suggestion. He didn't want to destroy their friendship before he got his chance to make it something more.

She released his hand, picked up her coffee, and wistfully brushed her lips over her cup. "The beach."

He relaxed and softly said, "Yeah, why not? We could celebrate your birthday there. I believe it's coming up."

"It is. I'll think about it. I've got to go." She stood up.

"I'll take you home." He stood up with her.

The ride was quiet while he drove her home. She stretched out in the passenger seat and napped. He hoped that she would consider his suggestion. It would be nice to spend time with her without everyone's eyes on them.

CHAPTER 16

In mid-October, Terri relented to Carter's request to go away for a long weekend to Savannah. She wasn't handling the stress of the separation well, and he felt that a change of scenery would help her relax. He arrived at her aunt's house around 3:00 p.m.

She peeked out of the window and he got out of the car. She opened the door for him.

"All set?" he asked.

"Yep."

He noticed her travel bag on the floor in the foyer and picked it up. "I'll take this for you."

They settled in the car and took off.

"Do you have a preference on music?" he asked.

"Not really." She said. "Where are we staying?"

"In a two-bedroom cottage near downtown Savannah. There are so many events in town that I thought it would be more interesting than staying on the beach. We'll ride out to Tybee Island on Saturday morning for sunrise. It's beautiful."

"So, you've been to Savannah before?"

"Oh yes," he beamed. "There's so much to do. I'm really glad you agreed to come."

***

"We're almost there." Carter said.

Terri roused from her nap. "Ugh," she groused and covered her nose. "What's that smell?"

"Paper factory," he chuckled. "The smell will die down when we get closer to town."

"Wow, I hope so."

Fifteen minutes later, they arrived at the reservation office. After retrieving the keys, they went to the cottage and opened the door.

"Nice place." Terri exclaimed. "Have you stayed here before?"

"No. This place was recommended by a friend. I'll let you pick which room you want, and I'll take the other one."

She selected the room on the left-hand side of the hall. He dropped her bags off next to her bed.

"It's late and I'm turning in." He enwrapped her in a light, shallow hug. "Sweet dreams."

"Goodnight." She said, sweetly.

***

Carter was seated at the breakfast table. He'd left the cottage early and picked up pastries and coffee for breakfast. He'd allowed her to sleep in so she would be well rested.

He heard her door open and the shower shortly thereafter. Twenty minutes later, she appeared in the kitchen. He stood up to greet her.

"I've got a lot of plans on the itinerary today. I hope you rested well and have comfortable shoes."

"I slept very well." She picked up the coffee on the end of the table closest to her. "Is this mine?"

"Yea." He motioned for her to take it. "Cream cheese Danish. One of your favorites."

She picked up the sweet treat and sat at the table.

Carter also sat down.

"Ooh, this is a good one. You're spoiling me."

"It's your birthday weekend. We're friends and you deserve to have fun. It's not every day you turn twenty-one again." He winked.

"Thank you." She giggled and took a bite of her Danish. "What's the first stop on the itinerary?"

"Cathedral of St. John the Baptist," he stated.

"You're taking me to church?" she asked. "I'm surprised. We've never discussed faith before."

He took a sip of his coffee and finished his Danish. "I attended Catholic schools although my family was Methodist. My family wanted a better education for all of us. I have five sisters and I'm the only son."

"Wow. She beamed and was amazed at his revelation. "Faith is important to you then?"

"It is," he replied. "It's been a struggle between Catholicism and the Methodist Christian doctrine. I pray every day for wisdom and understanding."

"That is so wonderful that you practice your faith and pray. I would love to go to the Cathedral. I have a few things to pray about and this may give me inspiration while working on my troubles."

"Beautiful churches always inspire me as do beautiful women," he stated.

"If that was a compliment for me, thank you." She lightly hugged him. "Give me ten minutes. I've got to finish my hair and makeup."

***

"What a day." She said as they entered the cottage that evening. "I don't remember ever doing that much walking."

He closed the door behind him. "I hope I didn't creep you out by taking you to churches, cemeteries and ghost tours."

"I didn't know you were into that. I love ghost stories." She set her purse and packages down on the kitchen table.

He had a few bags of his own and set them down too. "The next time we come. We'll go to Colonial Park Cemetery. There's not enough time with what I have planned for tomorrow."

"You're already planning the next trip?" she grinned. "This one isn't over yet."

His brown cheeks reddened. He was overly excited about this trip and didn't want it to end.

"Did you enjoy dinner?" he asked and tried to compose himself, changing subjects to something safer.

"You're blushing. That's cute." She said and approached him. She brushed her hand against his cheek.

He took a few steps back. "Stop, Terri. I'm cool."

She laughed. "I don't think I've ever seen you blush."

"Ah man." He raised his eyes up towards the ceiling. "Let this one go, please."

"Okay." She giggled. "I'm going to change and watch TV for a little while. Do you want to watch something together?"

"Sure."

She picked up her purse and walked down the hall.

Damn.

She's making this difficult for me to be a gentleman.

He changed to comfortable sweats and a T-shirt. He went into the living room and she was still in her room. He sat on the couch and turned on the TV.

She came out five minutes later in a short-sleeved, knee-length nightgown. She sat on the couch shoulder to shoulder next to him.

"What did you find to watch?"

He handed the remote control to her. "I'll watch whatever you want."

She surfed the channels and found the movie *"The Hunt for Red October."*

He twitched.

She was too close.

He stood up.

"What's wrong?" Terri asked.

"It's late. I thought you might want more room on the couch if you want to lie down." He went back to the bedroom and found extra blankets. He laid one over Terri and sat in the cushioned chair next to the couch.

You're a married woman and I'm a single man that's in love with you. You're safer on the couch by yourself.

"Can you see the TV?" she asked.

"Yea, girl. I'll be asleep in a few. I may catch most of this movie but if I nod out, goodnight, love."

"Goodnight, Carter."

CHAPTER 17

"Happy Birthday." He hugged her.

"Thank you." She offered her cheek in against his lips. "You've been out already."

"I have. I didn't want you to be hungry." He released her and offered her the box on the table. "I've got coffee for you and Krispy Crème doughnuts."

"That's thoughtful. Thank you." She picked up the treat and took a bite. "Mmm. That's good. Still hot."

He took a seat at the table and she sat cattycorner from him.

"I thought we'd go to the beach this morning. The weather will be sunny and warm. Did you bring a swimsuit?"

"I did but I don't think I'm wearing it."

Damn!

No chance to see her sexy body.

Probably best she doesn't wear it. I'd have a hard time keeping the soldier from saluting her.

"We won't stay long. I want to get there early before it gets too hot."

She savored another bite from the doughnut. "Mmm. I haven't had one of these in a long time."

"What do you want to do afterwards? We could do the Riverboat cruise, a comedy club, a nightclub, lunch dinner, theater…anything you want. Just name it." He offered her the brochures on the table of several local attractions. "I picked a few of these up on the way in."

"There's so much to do. We only have today and then back to reality. We have to come back—" she stopped herself from continuing her sentence. He grinned and nodded.

***

"That was fun." Terri slipped off her shoes as soon as they arrived back to the cottage.

They'd had dinner on the Savannah Riverboat Cruise line.

"I've been on a ship before but not a dinner cruise. I'm glad we tried that."

"I'm glad you had a good time. I did too," he said. He walked over to the kitchen table and emptied his pockets.

"I'm turning in," she said and walked down the hall.

Carter softly called out to her, "Terri."

She spun around.

His brown eyes and his curly locks softened against the dim lighting in the living room.

She was unable to move any further down the hall.

He took a few steps toward her. Her mouth fell open and she let out a silent gasp.

She swooned.

He rushed over to catch her.

He secured her in his strong muscular arms and held her close.

"Baby, it's okay. I'm here," he whispered and swaddled her limp body in his arms.

"It's just. I—" she stammered and clutched his back tightly and pressed her head against his chest.

He held her close and hoped that she wouldn't shove him away. His dreams of holding her in his arms were fulfilled. She was soft, delicate and beautiful, just like he imagined.

She tilted her head and raised her lips within inches of his. He pressed his lips against hers delicately enough to express his desire. He refrained from releasing the rest of his intense passion. He didn't want to scare her away.

She pulled him closer and parted her lips. She lightly stroked the inseam of his pants. Her sensual touch ignited his passion for her.

His lips pressed against her neck in small kisses behind her ear. His hands traveled down her back and rounded her behind with a light squeeze.

She fingered the inside of his suit jacket and lifted it off his shoulders. It landed on the floor behind him on the baseboard. She unbuttoned his shirt and lifted his tee. Her fingers explored through the hairs on the center of his chest.

He unzipped the back of her black, knee-length dress. Still pressed between their bodies, he gave space between them and allowed it to drop to the floor.

She pushed him back slightly. Her forehead creased, and her lips pursed with concern.

"We can't do this. I-I-I'm not divorced."

His words flowed in her ear like the Savannah River on a hot summer day. "Let's not worry about that now."

Her platonic friend disappeared and out came his raw and natural primal male instincts ready to capture his woman. He wasn't about to let her go without a fight for her mind, body, and soul.

She glided her fingers up and down his back and pinched his well-toned muscles. He unbuckled his belt and unzipped his pants. The clothes puddled on the floor around his ankles. He stepped into the doorway of her room and encouraged her to follow him to the side of her bed.

His right hand unhooked her coral lace bra and his left hand slid down her low-rise panties. Her well-toned, sexy body was exposed and he yearned to satisfy her.

The man she married, whatever the hell his name was, didn't know how lucky he'd been.

Carter was glad Ricky hadn't seen sense.

He pulled the sheets and laid her down between them. She allowed him to spread her legs apart just enough to receive him.

His strong and muscular hands moved down her torso and up between her thighs. Her body temperature rose, and she writhed beneath him until he settled between her thighs.

"Oh," she moaned.

His enticing movements fanned the flames of desire that burned within her. He nibbled on her ear while her back arched and wriggled in a silent plea for him to quench her sexual thirst.

His fingers brushed her skin like a slow burning fire torching each follicle of hair along the way. Each kiss was more powerful and electrifying. She dug her nails in his arms and flinched joyfully with every touch. He lifted her thigh and slowly penetrated her.

His deliberate thrusts were met with her passion. He slowly increased his movements. She moaned in pure ecstasy and beamed in orgasmic delight.

She cooed and tremored. He groaned and quaked.

When she came, he flew with her.

When they came back to reality, she was still holding him in her arms.

***

A few hours later, he woke up with her still in his arms. The ultimate pleasure with her was worth the wait. Her acceptance of his advances confirmed what he suspected. She was no longer in love with Ricky and was open to starting a new relationship with him.

A man like Ricky didn't deserve to have a woman like her, and he sure as hell didn't know how to please her.

Carter's lovemaking with Terri was beyond any spiritual and intimate encounter that he'd ever had. He continued to caress her body while she rested and wondered how he let her get away in the first place. He assuredly would not make the same mistake twice.

His release of his feelings for her soothed the ache he carried in his heart for years. Her sweet scent of vanilla almond remained ingrained in his brain.

But she laid next to him still married to the wrong man.

CHAPTER 18

It was mid-morning and time to get on the road back to Atlanta. Carter packed his bag while Terri was taking a shower.

He knocked on the bathroom door. "Terri?"

"Yes?" She turned off the water.

"Let's get breakfast on the way back to Atlanta."

"Okay."

He sat in the kitchen and watched the headline news while she finished dressing. He went to the bedroom just as she came out of the bathroom.

"You okay?" he asked.

"I'm fine." She tightened her bathrobe. "I'll be ready in fifteen."

"Okay. Cool."

The only sound on the ride back to Atlanta was the jazz music cd. She peered out the window and watched the passing scenery.

He broke the silence.

"There's a breakfast place on the right. Is this okay with you?"

She glanced over at him and agreed. "That's fine."

He relaxed and hoped she wasn't upset about last night. He was reluctant to mention the conclusion of their weekend getaway. Taking advantage of a vulnerable woman wasn't his style.

They arrived at Cracker Barrel and were seated by the hostess. The waitress came by a few minutes later.

"I'm your waitress, Trini." She laid the menus on the table. "What a cute couple. Coffee?"

Startled, Terri's mouth flew open.

He interjected before she could respond. "Thank you. She's my better half. Regular coffee for the both of us."

"I'll be right back for your order." She left the table.

He motioned for her to pick up her menu.

"What the—" she demanded.

"Do you know what you want?" he asked and dismissed her concern.

"I'm not sure that I do." She snapped.

He looked up and met her angry stare. "I know exactly what I want." He refused to look away, watched as the anger slowly faded from her gaze, her lips parted on her quickened breath.

He was *not* referring to breakfast.

"You do?" "I do." He asserted his answer in a firm tone.

The waitress returned to take their order.

"Ladies first." Carter motioned for her to speak.

"I'm very hungry. I'll have Uncle Herschel's breakfast."

"I'll have the Country Boy breakfast." He handed both of their menus to the waitress.

"Coming right up."

Terri waited until the woman walked away and then confronted him. "What do you mean, you *know what you want*? And what happened between us last night?"

He was captivated by her curious brown eyes.

He hadn't fully understood himself what transpired between them. He knew better than to seduce a married woman into making love with him.

He answered her question nonchalantly. "I don't know."

"I'm still married to Ricky."

He didn't need that reminder. "I know," he replied. He slowly inhaled and released his breath. He wished that she were single.

"What are we going to do?" she asked.

Breakfast arrived before he could answer.

"We take this a day at a time." He answered after the waitress left. "You're under a lot of pressure. I don't want to contribute to it."

She declared. "You already have."

"Did you at least enjoy your weekend?" he asked. She met his gaze, "It was perfect."

***

They arrived at her home late Sunday evening. He brought her luggage inside and watched her every move as she settled in. He stood by the doorway ready to bid his goodnight. As she approached him, he took her hand and pulled her into a light hug.

She whispered in his ear. "You can't stay here. My aunt's sleeping."

"I know."

He picked up her hand, which still bore Ricky's wedding rings. He gently pulled off the rings and handed them to her.

She focused on the rings then clasped them in her hand. He placed his hand on her back and whispered in her ear. "You're no longer in love with him. You've moved out and moved on. Give the brother his rings back."

She gasped.

He brushed his lips across her cheek.

"I'll do that."

He took a step back and nodded. His dark eyes were settled directly on hers. He made the statement, but her response was unexpected. This would be the first step in undoing a marriage that should have never happened in the first place.

He bent to kiss her, and she pushed him away.

"I need more time to think about this."

He released her and agreed. As he turned to leave, she held his arm and whispered in his ear.

"Goodnight."

***

He took his belongings inside his house, bare walls, simple furniture, and modest style.

He wondered what it would be like for her to live here.

He would love to see her every single day when he walked in the door. She'd decorated her own home with simple tastes in earthy red tones.

He went into the master bedroom and put his travel bag on his unmade king-size bed. He wasn't the world's greatest housekeeper, but could find everything he owned.

He wondered if they would ever return to Savannah again together.

He stared at the clock and was hypnotized by its movements.

His doorbell rang.

He opened the door and there she was.

The expression on her face was of a panicked and lost woman. Her purse was in her hand and her lips were slightly parted. He took the purse from her hand, which must have weighed a ton at that moment, and ushered her inside his house.

He led her into the kitchen and placed her purse aside. She sat down. "Do you want some coffee?"

She drew a deep breath and slowly exhaled. "Yes, thank you."

He brewed the pot.

He knew that a talk was coming and wasn't sure what to expect. He brought her a cup and sat down next to her. "Are you okay?"

He was worried that he'd moved too soon.

Terri was here but she wasn't comfortable, and he wanted her to relax.

Her eyes were darkened with pain. "Yes, I'm fine."

She sipped her coffee carefully. She appeared as if her mind were thousands of miles away and yet she'd come and sat at his kitchen table.

At least for now.

"We can't continue to do this. It's not right. I'm not divorced."

"I know." He moved his chin down slowly.

She stood up and walked to the door without a key or purse in her hand.

He followed her.

She turned her back to him. She stood there with open arms. Too stunned to move and nothing to say.

Carter knew she wasn't ready to leave. Instinctively he made his next move.

He brushed his hand against her hair and wrapped his arm around her waist. He tilted her head back and delivered kisses in and behind her ear. She curved her body to meld into his.

If she didn't hear his body call out to her, she did now. His warm breath and wet tongue traced the outline of her ear. He played to win at all costs and threw the consequences out the window. There was no way for her to resist his advances. At least not tonight.

He led her to his first-floor master. She wasn't getting away from him again.

Making love with her three times was no mistake. His longtime friendship with Terri was something more.

CHAPTER 19

Carter arrived home from work late Wednesday evening. He opened the garage door and Terri's car was parked inside.

He'd given her keys to his home a few weeks ago.

She was sitting on the living room couch, reading, when he walked in.

"Hi, love." He leaned over and kissed her cheek.

She laid down the book and blushed. "Hi."

"I have a fraternity meeting tonight. Greg's picking me up."

"I'll stay for a little while for the peace and quiet. I'll probably be gone when you get back."

He sat down next to her. "Do you want me to stay? I'm here if you need me."

"No," she shook her head. "Go have fun."

"He'll be here in another hour. Is there any leftover lasagna?" He stood up and went into the kitchen.

She stood up and followed him. "There is. I'll heat it up for you. Go unwind."

He hugged her and whispered in her ear. "I think you don't want me to burn down the house."

She smacked his arm. "Get out of here."

He kissed her and tasted the strawberry flavored lip gloss. "Mmm. Good. I like that flavor."

"Now I don't have it anymore. You licked it off. I have to apply more." She teased.

He flexed his arm and pressed her tightly against his chest. His lips dabbed softly against her earlobe. The air he exhaled warmly breezed through her ear. "Baby, I want you."

"You do." She smiled coyly. She lifted her hand and caressed his cheek.

"I do," he wrapped his arm around her waist.

"What about your meeting?" she asked and slowly unbuttoned his shirt.

"We have time," he pressed a soft kiss to her lips.

He released her, clasped his hand on her wrist and pulled the kitchen chair from the table. His eyes lowered towards the chair and she sat on it with her legs crossed.

He opened his mouth and placed her pointer finger on his tongue. He swirled his tongue around it and nipped it from the base of her hand to her fingernail.

He held her wrist and traced her pointer finger down the center of his chest to the top of his belt.

"You're a damn freak!" she exclaimed. "I'm surprised to find this out about you."

He gently tugged her wrist. He glided his hand up her arm, across her shoulder and pushed a few strands of hair away from her ear. He placed his thumbs on her eyelids and gently closed them. He gently pressed his lips against each one.

His tongue traced down her forehead to the tip of her nose. Her lips parted, and he lowered his tongue to the top of her lip. "Come play with me, baby."

She panted noisily and jumped up from the chair. "Damn! You're hot."

She jerked his belt and he arched his back. She unbuckled him and unzipped his pants. He popped the top button on his jeans and they dropped to the floor.

His hand rounded her behind. His mouth covered hers and his hungry tongue swirled around hers.

She pushed him back, jerked the elastic on his boxers, and freed the hardened rod inside. She took a hold of his cock with one hand and stroked his marbles with the other.

"Shit," he exclaimed. His excitement was close to a euphoric state. He tugged at her jogging pants, she pulled them down, and he palmed her buttock, turned her to face the kitchen table, bend over its top.

She extended her arms and gripped the edge for leverage.

He glided his fingers along her crease.

"Ooh," she moaned.

The head of his rod followed the path that his fingers traced.

Her butt jiggled, and she squirmed.

He got on his knees, licked her crease, and popped her ass with a smack.

"Ah," she cried out.

He stood, pushed her legs farther apart, and entered with slow moving thrusts.

"Do you feel me, baby?" he moaned and glided in and out of her.

"Yes-yes-yes," she huffed.

Beads of perspiration rained on their skin. She keened, begged for more as his thrusts grew faster and he reached around to her front to thumb her clit. Her muscles tightened around him, and Carter followed Terri over into the bliss of orgasm. They laid over the hard wood, trying to catch their breath, until his spent cock slipped from her and his legs weren't so rubbery. He moved first to find a cloth to help her clean up, knelt before her to set her clothes to right, worshiped up at her from his knees while she ran her fingers through his hair. "I'm never letting you go," he whispered.

***

Carter left the house though his garage.

"Whose car was that? I know you don't have two." Greg asked.

He realized that he should have left through the front door instead.

"A friend." Carter answered. He fastened his seatbelt.

"I haven't seen you much lately." Greg's face lit up with a revelation. "That's Terri's car. I thought I recognized it. The last time I saw it was at the party at her house."

Carter sat back and remained silent while Greg pulled out of the driveway.

"Dog! You didn't." Greg exclaimed.

Carter glanced over at him.

"Oh hell naw. This is some messed up shit. Do you remember when I dated Bambi?"

Carter answered "Yea. I'm glad that's done."

"You know she just had a baby."

Carter jerked back and creased his eyebrows.

"Not mine, dog." Greg exclaimed. "You won't believe who. I took a paternity test last week. It's not mine."

"Yo, brother. Be glad. That would have been an eighteen-year sentence. I didn't like her."

"Guess who the father is?"

Carter cocked his head and waited for the response.

"Ricky Burke."

"And how the hell did you find that out?" Carter exclaimed.

He remembered the Valentine's dance. He'd known it was Ricky, but not who the woman was. Bambi couldn't have been the woman's real name anyways. The white girl's phone number on the phone. The details of the report from the Fellows

Detective Agency. Bambi. Diane. They were the same person. "Damn, Greg."

"I know. And you have his wife in your house. Ain't this some shit? You can't make this up. I'm selling this story to Spike Lee and make me some money."

He was floored by Greg's revelation. He was sure that Terri didn't know about the baby or Bambi. She only knew that Ricky was cheating. It was a matter of time before she found out. He didn't want to see her hurt.

***

He hadn't seen Terri in the past week and was worried about her. He called and left several messages without any answer. He was concerned that she may have gotten into an altercation with her soon to be ex-husband. He stopped by her house after work on Friday.

He was in the driveway when she pulled up. She pulled her car in next to his. She got out and they both stood and faced each other behind their respective cars.

"Why are you here?" she demanded.

"I think we should talk."

She invited him into the house and they sat on the couch.

He asked, "Why won't you take or return any of my calls? If I offended you in any way, I really didn't mean to."

She shook her head. "I shouldn't have gone to Savannah with you. That was a huge mistake."

"I didn't think so. I wanted you to relax."

"I've hired an attorney to handle my divorce."

He was surprised.

She hadn't mentioned Ricky in a while. "Good."

"Good!" she huffed. "Is that what you have to say to me?"

"Terri. I love you. I want you to be happy. He's not right for you."

"I've moved from one drama to another." She jumped up from the couch and slammed the bathroom door.

Carter got up and followed her. He knocked on the bathroom door. "Are you okay?"

After she flushed the toilet, she came out of the bathroom. She folded her arms against her chest. "No, I'm not."

"What's up?" he asked. "I can't help if I don't know what's going on."

"This is what's up." She went back to the bathroom and handed him a plastic thermometer with a plus sign on it.

After inspecting the device, his eyes swept her up and down. He hoped that she would confirm his suspicions. "Do you have something to tell me?"

"This is your baby, Carter. The doctor's office confirmed that I'm pregnant."

Wonderment filled his face. He was elated. This was an unexpected connection to her.

He grinned like a proud papa. He grabbed her and kissed her on the lips. "This is great. You're having my baby."

"No, it's not great!" She scowled. "I'm married and carrying another man's baby. I'm not ready to be a mother. And I'm certainly not gonna be shacking up with the baby-daddy who is the whole reason I'm in this mess in the first place! I'll be doing this alone."

"You won't do this alone. I'll be here with you."

She shouted angrily, "What are you going to tell Ricky? Are you going to tell him that you got his wife pregnant?"

He didn't know how to answer her. He only thought of himself. He knew Ricky didn't deserve her, but this was not the outcome he expected.

She pointed to the door. "It's time for you to go."

CHAPTER 20

Carter was restless that night.

His intimate nights with Terri produced an unanticipated result. Carter remembered Mona's words from the wedding.

Expect the unexpected.

Although he didn't plan for this to happen, he felt that fate had intervened. He often thought of the night in Savannah where their souls first intertwined. There was no other woman on the face of the earth that he would freely give his heart and soul.

She was upset that she was pregnant, but he would work hard to get her to come around. His brain wrestled with a plan to have her completely.

The first step was to keep the dialogue open with her and communicate with her more often. During their conversations over the past year, he learned active and intimate conversation was very important to her. He believed this important information would help them become closer friends and lovers.

He'd waited on her for three years. Now he was very close to having her.

He heard ringing sounds.

"I must be dreaming."

He glanced at the clock and it was 2:00 a.m. He tried to reach it but instead knocked it off the nightstand. He realized that it wasn't the clock but the doorbell.

Whoever this fool was had better have a good excuse for waking him up early this morning.

He put on his robe and answered the door.

He peeked through the pane and Terri was standing there. He flicked on the lights and opened the door. He was elated to see her.

"What do I owe the pleasure of this visit?"

She brushed past him and entered the home. He could feel she was frustrated and in no mood to play games with him. "I couldn't sleep. We have to talk about child support."

Terri standing in the middle of his home in the early morning was like a dream come true. She paced the floor in his living room with nervous intensity.

"I wouldn't have to pay child support if we got married." He said nonchalantly.

She stopped pacing and placed her hand over her chest. She widened her eyes and the rest of her face had a horrified expression.

"You want to avoid child support by getting married!" she shouted. "You've got to be kidding me! I'm still married to another man."

Although Carter was drowsy, he was now fully awake. His proposal to Terri was long overdue. He wanted Terri and their baby with him on a permanent basis. She took his proposal as an escape from child support.

He attempted to ease her concerns. "No that's not why I want to marry you, Terri, you mean more to me than that. Let's talk more in the living room."

She glared at him. "After the bathroom stop. This will have to wait." Terri went to the bathroom, returned to the living room, and sat next to Carter on the couch.

He faced her for their important discussion.

"I want you and my baby here with me. There is plenty of room."

She responded, "I can't live here. I'm not in love with you. I fell for you in a moment of weakness and I should have been smart enough to remember to take my birth control."

"Have you ever thought to ask me how I feel?"

She waved him away. "It doesn't matter. The baby is my problem."

He took her hand, held it to his heart. He lifted his other hand and caressed her cheek. He cupped her chin and expressed his feelings for her without hesitation. The desperate appeal in his eyes blazed through her.

"My soul is reaching out to you. Our baby is a result of me completely giving myself to you and your warm reception. Terri, I've been in love with you for a long time. I thought that you would have noticed that by now. I knew your marriage to Ricky was a mistake and he didn't deserve to have you."

She protested, "I can't start another marriage Carter, I just..."

He leaned in and pressed his lips against her in pure unadulterated passion. Waves of desire torched through his muscles. He stood up and assisted her to her feet.

"I love you. I want you here with me. If you aren't ready to get married, then at least stay here with me."

She was unable to resist the passionate kisses pressed against her skin. She acquiesced to his advances and moaned. "I don't know. I don't know what to say."

He half-whispered between kisses. "Don't say anything right now just feel the heat of my passion."

"Oh," she murmured. "Feeling your passion has gotten me pregnant."

Carter slowly placed more kisses down the back of her shoulders. He coaxed her into his bedroom and she obediently followed.

An hour later, they nestled under the covers. He whispered in her ear. "I need you here with me more than you will ever know."

She placed his hand on her stomach. He knew that they were connected forever.

CHAPTER 21

Carter sat in the living room early evening and waited for Terri's arrival. He heard her pull into the garage.

"Carter, where are you?"

"In the living room." He stood up to greet her. He moved to give her a hug but refrained. The scowl on her face indicated that she wasn't in a good mood.

She took off work to meet her attorney. Her brother-in-law recommended Christopher Sharpley. Today was her third visit to his office.

He wanted to go with her but knew this was something she had to do on her own. From the expression on her face, it must not have gone well.

"It will take six to eight months to get divorced. This is a big mess. I should have never married that man." She dropped her purse and keys on the kitchen chair.

He dismissed her concerns. "Don't worry. I'm here supporting you every step of the way."

"That's not the biggest news." She grabbed a bottle of water from the refrigerator. "You want one?"

"Yea." He accepted the cold bottle.

"I had lunch with Lisa at Dreamland Bar-B-Que."

"How is she?" He asked and wasn't sure where this conversation was going.

"She's fine. She told me that Ricky has a newborn daughter. He took a blood test. It was 100% positive that it was Ricky's baby. She also told me that there was someone else that took the blood test."

"It was Greg," he stated.

Her eyes lit up with surprise. "How did you know that?"

He shrugged, "Greg told me,"

"What else did he tell you?" she demanded.

He breathed a heavy sigh. "The woman Ricky got pregnant was Greg's girlfriend. The one from the Valentine's Dance."

"Unbelievable!" she shouted. "What else do you know?"

His eyes were filled with sorrow. He got up from the table and brought her a large manila envelope. She glanced at him with a curious expression. She opened it and gasped. She couldn't believe what she saw.

"Where did you get these?" Terri demanded.

"I hired a private detective after you told me about your phone calls."

Inside the envelope were pictures of Ricky with several different women. Terri recognized some of the trysts were on dates that he was supposed to be out of town on a business trip. It had the paternity test of Ricky and Bambi's baby.

His report was very thorough.

"What were you going to do with this?" Terri asked angrily.

"I don't know."

She took the envelope and pictures and tossed it across the room. She stood up, waved her finger in his face and yelled at him. "Why did you keep this from me? I thought I could trust you."

He backed up from her with open arms. "I couldn't tell you Terri. It couldn't come from me."

Terri kept her finger in his face. "You knew my life was falling apart and you never said a word. I'm beginning to think you enjoyed my suffering."

He silently stood beside her and allowed this drama to unfold. "I hated to see you go through this. I couldn't be the one to tell you." He said in a low tone. "You agreed to be with him for better or worse. I was protecting you."

She scowled, "I just left a man with a double life and I'm now with a man who hides things from me for my own protection. We have to be honest with each other in order for this to work. I expect you to be honest with me."

"Yes, ma'am." He reached for her hand and she snatched it away. "You deserve honesty from me. It's a shame you had to go through this. You're an amazing woman and handle adversity well. Please don't ask me to always be honest with you because I don't want to see you hurt."

"You were out with him. You knew what he was doing. Didn't you?"

Carter was silent as she spouted her anger. "Terri, you're pregnant. Calm down."

"I will not calm down," she shouted. "I expected better from you. My sister shouldn't be the one that gave me this news, not if you knew it first."

"Wait, let's talk about this."

"Now you want to talk about this." She marched over to the kitchen chair and grabbed her purse and keys. "I'm getting the hell out of here."

He tried to block her from leaving but she pushed him out of the way. She screeched out of the driveway.

CHAPTER 22

It was Christmas day. Dinner was at Doug and Lisa's house. Greg invited him to tag along. He knew that Terri would be there. He welcomed the chance to see her.

Greg arrived to pick him up for dinner. Carter was silent while he sat in the car and thought about Terri's pregnancy. He desperately wanted her to marry him and they become a family. Terri was still disappointed with him about his knowledge of Ricky's affairs.

Greg interrupted his thoughts.

"Terri's parents are going to be there. Are you ready for that drama?" Greg glanced over at Carter and waited for his response. Carter slowly came out of his deep thought and felt helpless about his fate.

"Yes, I'm ready. She told her parents about us. She's still upset with me. I'm trying to get her to come around."

Greg watched his partner's far away gaze. "You've got it bad. Everyone will know it when you walk in the door."

They arrived at Doug's mansion. Carter could smell the aroma of turkey and sweet potato pie as he walked in the door. Doug took their coats and led them into the kitchen. All of Lisa's family were socializing and having a good time.

Terri looked up from the table. Her sexy brown eyes blazed right through his heart.

Her berry colored lips silently breathed his name as he walked inside the door. She sat back in her chair and her mouth parted even wider. She rose from the table still unable to speak.

He strolled over to her and sang these words to her. "Merry Christmas, Terri."

Everyone in the room witnessed the intensity of this exchange. He was in love with Terri and her family instantly knew it. Her eyes were burned with emotion. She placed her hand over her heart and softly breathed her response. "Thank you, Carter"

Her whisper of his name melted all four chambers in his heart. She was the mother of his child and the keeper of his soul. He would do anything she wanted. All she had to do was ask.

His soft expression of free love for her sent a message to her heart. A piece of his soul was intertwined with hers growing a new life. A life that would always bind them together in the forever kind of sense.

Ann stood beside Terri and glared at him. She firmly spoke to her daughter. "Terri, can you assist me for a moment?"

She followed her mother and Carter silently watched her leave.

Doug clapped his shoulder. "Let's go to the entertainment room."

"Sure." He shrugged off the encounter and followed Doug.

A half hour later, Carter was talking with Doug and Joey and felt her presence when she stood in the doorway. He put down his drink and his heart raced fast as he walked towards her.

Doug discreetly motioned for the guests to leave the room. Carter didn't take his eyes off Terri and noticed they were soon to be the only ones in the room. He caught Doug's eye when he looked back and nodded in appreciation for the private time with Terri.

He brushed his face against hers with the slight prickly feel of his beard. It was a scratchy bristly sensation against her soft skin. His soft lips cushioned the blow against her ear. "How are you feeling?"

The brother had a style like no other. If she weren't in the middle of a Christmas party, she would take the brother for a drive and she didn't mean in a car. "I'm fine, Carter."

It was all that he could do to restrain himself from taking her out of here. Now that he'd had her, it was impossible not to think of her every day, every hour, and every moment of time. She had a brother twisted in places that he didn't know he had. He had to have her, and no was not an option.

"When can we talk?"

"Soon. I'm going to help Lisa with dinner."

"Not yet."

He reached in his pocket and offered her the small box in his hand. She stared at it and clasped it in her hand. She was unsure about opening it because she knew what was in it.

"Not now," she said and shook her head.

"Terri, please."

She opened the box slowly and gasped at the contents. He gave her a two-carat marquee shaped diamond engagement ring.

"I do want to marry you."

She closed the box and gave it back to him. He took her in his arms and cuddled her.

"Not now. I'm not ready," she breathed.

He was hurt that she rejected his proposal again. He didn't want to push her into another marriage and he didn't want to lose her either. He knew that it was a matter of time before she accepted his ring. He sadly put it away in his pocket. "Promise to sit with me at dinner."

Tears streamed down her face. He knew her heart was torn over her feelings for him. She needed more time to think about it.

She squeezed his arms and kissed him. "I will."

***

After the table had been blessed and dinner served, they sat silently next to each other and glanced over at one another on occasion.

"Is there anything that I can do for you?" he asked.

"No, thank you."

She forked through her plate but ate very little. He wanted to encourage her to eat more but he was in enough trouble with her as it was. His eyes were filled with sadness and remorse. He brushed his face against her ear. "What are you doing later on?"

She sighed. "I don't know. This is Christmas. It's beginning to be the worst one that I've ever had." She grabbed the saltshaker and sprinkled it over her mashed potatoes.

He wiped his mouth. "Don't say that. We have a chance to be together and I didn't have this chance last year."

"How did you get here?"

"Greg drove me."

"As soon as dinner is over, we're leaving. This is too much stress for me."

He reached under the table and squeezed her hand. "I didn't come to hurt you."

"I know," she murmured.

An hour after dinner, Terri went to the kitchen to take leftover Christmas dinner home. Carter stood beside the doorway while she packed up the food. Her mother was sitting at the table talking to Lisa. She stood up to help Terri.

"Are you okay?" Ann asked with concern in her voice.

"Yes, Mom; Carter and I are leaving to talk."

Ann folded her arms and glared over her daughter's shoulder at Carter, "Don't make any rash decisions."

Terri hugged her mother. "I won't, Mom. Merry Christmas. You will have another grandchild next year."

Carter and Terri bid everyone goodnight before they left for the evening. He walked with Terri to her car. "Do you want me to drive?"

"I can drive my own car," she snapped.

"Okay," he shrugged.

***

She sat down on one end of the couch and he sat down on the other. He lifted her legs into his lap. She grabbed the remote and turned on the TV.

"I'm exhausted." She said and surfed the channels.

He slid off her socks and flexed her feet between his hands. They were cold, and the friction warmed them up.

"Oh, I love that." She dropped the remote on the floor. He wiggled each toe individually and kissed the top of her feet. One hand cupped her heel and the other slid up her pants leg. He brushed her skin and squeezed the back of her calf.

"Oh no you don't. You're not getting out of this discussion." He moistened his lips and lifted her toes to his mouth. He sucked each one individually.

She writhed with delight. She unzipped her pants and pushed them down. He removed them and threw them on the floor. He pulled her tiger print panties down her legs. He hula hooped the garment around his finger before he tossed it across the room.

He pushed his tongue through his teeth and swiped it across the top of his lip. Her lips parted, and she gasped.

He lowered his face between her thighs and swirled his tongue around her core. He swished it faster and faster. She grabbed hold of his locks and wrapped her legs around his back.

"Yes-yes-yes." She panted. Beads of sweat popped across her brow. Her breasts bobbed up and down her chest and her eyes rolled upward to the ceiling.

He felt her body quake. She cooed, and panted. She pulled his locks to bring his face to hers. She kissed him in between gasps for air.

He whispered in her ear. "Let me be your ultimate lover."

"You already are." She moaned.

CHAPTER 23

Carter convinced Terri to spend New Year's away with him. He told her that it would be lucky if the both of them would be together to close out the old year and have a new beginning.

A large crowd atmosphere would dilute his focus on the two of them. Alone, in the woods with just the two of them was the perfect solution. He glanced over at her sitting in the passenger seat. They were finally together. A dream come true.

"You didn't say where we are going. I want my family to know." She frowned at him and voiced her concern.

"It's a surprise," he beamed. "You can tell them when we get there. How are you feeling?"

"I'm sensitive to certain foods so I'm learning what to avoid."

"I noticed." He chuckled. "No oatmeal for you."

"Sorry about that." She sighed. "I couldn't make it to the bathroom. Did I tell you how I found out I was pregnant?"

"No. You didn't." He flicked his turn signal on to change lanes.

"I was spending time with Lisa and Stacy. Doug came home. We chatted for a while and he told me that Lisa had extra pre-natal vitamins. I asked him: 'Why would I need those?' He then told me I was pregnant." Terri opened the grocery bag and grabbed the potato chips.

"How did he know?" Carter asked and picked up his water out of the cup holder. "I thought he was a lawyer."

"I don't know. Lisa had a stash of pregnancy tests in the bathroom and she told me to take one. I was sure he was wrong. That damn thing turned into a plus sign in the bathroom and I lost it. I was so shocked, I cried so loud that everyone knocked on the door to see if I was okay. It took me a while to calm down." She crunched a few chips and took a sip of her water.

He pressed a button and changed the song on the CD player to "Wait for Love" by Luther Vandross.

"I never thought about getting pregnant or having children. I believe I missed a few pills with all the stress going on with Ricky. You and I went to Savannah and we know what happened there."

Carter bobbed his head with the flow of the beat. Music was his world. He sang along with the song.

His singing voice was kryptonite for many women in his personal and professional life. He sang sparingly around Terri when they were alone. He wanted to develop their relationship in other areas.

He glanced over at her. She stopped eating her chips and stared at him. She was enwrapped in the sound of his voice.

"I love hearing you sing." She breathed. "I stand by the door when you're in the shower just to hear you."

"Thanks," he responded and focused on the road ahead. "I'll serenade you sometime. Not yet."

"Why?" she frowned. "Do I have to come every Wednesday night to hear you sing? I'm surprised you're not on tour. Noel's must be packed every Wednesday to hear you."

He laughed. "Not quite but close."

He squeezed her hand. "I want to reserve it for a special occasion." He winked at her. "Maybe this weekend."

"Ooh, I hope so," she breathed.

***

They arrived at their destination two hours later. Carter rented a cabin in Pine Mountain for the two of them for three days. Terri entered the cabin.

"This is cozy. I love the fireplace. Are we really here for three days?"

"Yes, Terri, I want to talk to you privately and uninterrupted. We need to plan the upcoming year."

He took dropped the suitcases inside the doorway. He went back to the car and brought back a shotgun and a pistol.

Terri appeared to be alarmed. "What's that?"

He dismissed her concerns. "We're in the woods, baby. Anything can happen. I have a conceal carry permit too."

She shook her head. "Okay. I hope you don't have to use that."

"Me too. I brought you something." He reached for one of the bags he brought in. He handed her a few books on pregnancy.

She laughed. "*What to Expect When You're Expecting.* Have you read any of these books?"

"I thought we would read them together this weekend." He had several bags of groceries so they could cook in the cabin. He emptied a few of the items on the counter.

She read over the titles. "You bought books on baby names?"

"I thought we'd do that this weekend too. There's a lot to a pregnancy. I will be with you every step of the way. I want us to both be educated and ask the right questions. Birthing a child can be life threatening. I am taking this pregnancy seriously."

He circled her in his arms and kissed her. "Why don't you get some rest? I'll have dinner ready in a while."

"Were you a boy scout? You have everything for well planned." She snickered.

"I was for a little while. Even though I'm a city boy, my dad insisted I learn a few survival skills which included learning how to use a firearm and hunt." He unbuttoned her coat and removed it from her shoulders.

She kissed him. "I'll see you in a little while."

***

He hoped the smell of the chicken vegetable stir-fry was strong enough to wake her up. He was facing the stove when he felt her head rest against his back and her arms circled around his waist. He lowered the temperature on the stove and faced her.

"I hope you rested well. Dinner is done if you're ready to eat."

She tilted her head back and looked up at him. "I'm starving. Do you want me to help?"

"Grab the plates. I hope you like it."

Dinner rolls and rice were already on the table. Terri noticed the box on the counter. She picked it up and inspected it. Her face brightened up. "Strawberry cheesecake from Elliot's! What a wonderful surprise. That's my favorite dessert."

He was elated that she liked his surprise. "If you remember, Elliot's was closed, and we didn't have a chance to eat there."

She opened the box and took a whiff of the dessert. "Ooh yummy."

Her eyes sparkled. "Since we are talking about favorite desserts. I seem to remember that you like brownies."

"You remembered that conversation." He opened a box on the same counter next to the cheesecake and brought it to her. Inside was a stack full of brownies.

She laughed. "How did I know that you would have those on hand?"

He slipped the stir-fry on their plates and the both sat down. Soft drinks, silverware, and water were on the table.

"How's your family? I'm sure they have a lot of questions."

"Mom and Dad weren't surprised that Ricky and I were having problems. After having that big wedding, they didn't expect that it wouldn't last an entire year. When I walked out, I was very relieved."

"Are your parents upset about your plans to move in with me?"

"They're not happy about that. They don't think that I should jump from one relationship to another. The shocker was telling them I was pregnant and that it wasn't Ricky's."

"Is it safe for me to meet them again? I know your mother was upset with me at Christmas."

"I want to wait a while on that. They are still digesting the fact that I'm getting divorced and pregnant with your baby. I'm not trying to hide you. I need some time for things to heal."

"I understand. I will wait until you are ready."

Carter knew that this must be a very stressful time for her and he didn't want to add any add to her troubles.

"I really was shocked to see you at Christmas dinner. I knew that Doug's friend Greg was coming and would be bringing a guest. I had no idea that you would be coming with him. My mother immediately figured out what was going on between us when you came into the room."

"There's no reason to hide my feelings for you now. He's gone. We have each other and our baby."

He reached across the table for her hand. She accepted his hand with a light squeeze. Carter caressed the length of her ringless finger.

"Are you ready for dessert?"

He got up from the table and sectioned a slice of cheesecake. He crooned Larry Graham's, "Just be my Lady."

She placed her hand over her heart and sighed. He sang a few of the words in her ear. She squealed.

He knelt down beside her, sectioned a piece of cheesecake with his fork, and fed it to her.

"Mmm." She licked her lips and he continued to sing. He forked the strawberry and grazed it against her lips. She opened her mouth and bit half of it.

"Just take my hand and I'll lead the way." He sang. He stood up and helped her rise to her feet. He swayed her from side to side. She followed his steps and laid her head on his chest.

He took her by the hand and crooned another song. He walked her to the living room and swayed her in his arms. He stepped back and twirled her. She squealed with delight.

He turned her back to him, lowered his pitch, and sang in her ear. She moaned as each note flowed in her ear.

He hugged her stomach. She placed her hands over his. He caressed her navel and his fingers smoothly traveled over her skin upwards to her breasts.

He stopped singing, planted his lips in the nape of her neck and squeezed her breasts.

"Tender." She moaned. He opened his hands, lifted her navy blue sweater and unclasped her bra. He cupped her breasts and fingered her nipples.

He lifted her sweater over her head. He moistened his lips, leaned over and pressed them against the nape of her back.

"Oh. Carter." She murmured.

His tongue traced the curvature of her spine until it reached the top of her shoulder blade.

He pulled her back to him and ever so slightly pushed down her sweat pants. She arched her back, while her sweats dropped to the floor. His hand rounded her behind, caressed the back of her thigh and lifted her leg out of the puddle of clothes.

"You're so damn hot." She breathed.

She jerked the top of his sweatpants and pulled him towards her.

"Let me show you what's hot."

He grabbed her hand, took her to the kitchen table, and lifted her on top of it. He rounded his arms under her legs, lowered his head and tasted the sweetness of her core.

"Take me to the mountain top." She grabbed his locks and gyrated with each swish of his tongue. He flicked his tongue rapidly.

She moaned, quaked and shivered.

He lifted her to a sitting position and she slid off the table.

She wrapped her arms around his shoulders and whispered in his ear. "I want you to sing to me while I'm downing you."

He smirked. If she downed him while he sang, he wouldn't be singing long.

She shoved down his sweat pants and pushed him back against the sink.

His shaft was erect and waved up and down. She grabbed a hold of it with both hands.

She pressed her body to his, breasts indented in his chest, lips to his and his shaft still in her hands. She squeezed him and whispered in his ear. "Sing."

He crooned his first note; she lowered her head and downed his shaft. Her actions caused him to sing off key.

"Keep singing," she ordered, "Or I'll stop."

He dutifully responded and soaked in the pleasure of her touch. He sang until he reached his euphoric state, gripped the counter and tremored.

He barely finished the last note, lifted her head and looked into her beautiful face.

"I adore you."

CHAPTER 24

It was a brisk and cold morning on New Year's Eve. The cabin was nice and toasty with the gas fireplace on.

He reached across the bed and she was gone. The smell of bacon woke his senses. He climbed out of bed and went into the kitchen. She was at the table drinking coffee and reading yesterday's news.

"Good morning, love." He kissed her cheek.

"Coffee's ready." She said.

He grabbed a cup, poured the fresh brew and sat next to her. "How'd you sleep?"

"Amazing." She said wistfully. "You crooned me to sleep. I don't think I've ever had that. I loved it." She took his hand and squeezed it. "Thank you."

He shrugged it off. "I wanted you to rest well. Do you want to go for a walk this morning?"

"Sure, but not far. I have to stay close to the bathroom. I'm not interested in going in the woods. Too cold for that."

"We'll go for a short walk around the lake. Dress extra warm. I'll bring the camping chairs.

***

"This looks like a good spot." Carter set up the chairs. They were ten minutes from the cabin. "We won't stay long. It's really cold."

She opened the thermos she was carrying and took a sip. "It is. I'm sure you'll warm me up when we get back."

He winked at her and laughed. "I will. It's part of the reason why I wanted to take you on a walk. We'll really enjoy the fireplace when we get back.

She took his hand. "I always imagined that by now, I would be a lawyer, married, with three kids, and have a house like Doug and Lisa's. It's funny how things pan out."

He motioned for her to sit in her chair. He sat next to her. "Sometimes what we plan is not what is supposed to happen."

"Why haven't you married yet?" she asked.

He thoughtfully responded. "I was waiting for the right woman. I didn't realize it until she was unavailable."

She suddenly had a revelation. She cocked her head towards him and squeezed his arm. "The wedding, Carter."

"What about it?"

"You told me at the rehearsal dinner that sometimes people that were meant to be together don't get together right away. I thought you were talking about Cynthia. You were talking about us, weren't you?"

He nodded, "I was. It was too late for you and me. You made your decision to marry Ricky. There was nothing I could do to stop it."

She set her coffee in the cup holder. "And that's why you wouldn't look at me when you hugged me at the wedding. I knew something was wrong. As I recall, you didn't dance with me either. I didn't pay attention to it at the time, but I remember it clearly."

His eyes were fixed on hers and his warm breath fogged in the air as he spoke. "I don't know how I got through your wedding. When Ricky asked me to be in it, I wanted to tell him no. I didn't have a good reason to give him. I couldn't tell him that I was in love with his bride. You expected me to give you a hug before I left. I couldn't look at you. You would have immediately known how I felt about you."

She nodded. "I really felt sorry for you. I thought you were still wrapped up in Cynthia. I knew that it was taking too long for you to get over her."

"I was over her long ago. She knew there was someone else and she didn't have a name. That created a lot of arguments and we finally called it quits. I speak to her occasionally. She's moved on with another man and she's happy. I told her that I was working on my own happiness with you."

Terri shook her head. Her cheeks reddened slightly, and she blinked rapidly.

He took her glove-covered hand and pressed it between his. "I've always been in love with you. You never looked my way. Once you put me in the friend zone, I knew it would be difficult for you to see me as more."

"It was hard to see you as more than a friend. I do have to admit when I thought you were interested in my cousin Stacy, I wasn't happy about it."

Carter laughed. "I know. I didn't catch on until Greg told me."

She grinned. "I wasn't exactly as discreet as I thought I was. Stacy teased me about it after the wedding. I was angry at first but then I realized she was right. I was just a tiny bit jealous."

He raised his eyebrows, "Tiny?"

She smacked his arm. "Quit teasing me."

"Okay," he snickered. "What made you open up to me? I'd given you plenty of hints that I was interested in you."

"Well," she sniffled and wiped her face with her scarf. The cold air reddened her cheeks. "At first I thought you were just being friendly. You've never made me feel uncomfortable around you like some of his other friends."

"You never suspected," he chuckled.

She acquiesced. "Yes and no. It was really evident when we had coffee earlier this year; I decided to just ignore it."

"Several of your friends and family called me out on it. I didn't want this to get back to you." He reached for her other hand. She gracefully placed it in his.

"Oh, it did." she continued. "My friends and family warned me about you. Truthfully, I enjoyed the attention. Ricky was never home, and you really took the time to listen to my dreams. You and I get along very well compared to my relationship with him."

He felt a chill, stood up and offered his hand to her. "Let's get back to the cabin so we can warm up."

***

"If I had known that a trip to Savannah would have caused me all this grief, I don't know if I would have gone." Terri covered her face. The natural birth movie she was watching was very graphic.

Her legs were in his lap and he caressed her shins. "Now Terri, if you hadn't come to Savannah, then we wouldn't be watching this cool movie. I will be there with you every step of the way."

She crinkled her eyebrows. "That's nice but I'm going to be the one screaming my head off."

He laughed. "Do you want to read some more or take a nap before lunch? I know you require a lot of rest."

"I'm comfortable here. I want to recline and read for a while."

He reached for the books on the table and handed them to her.

She tilted her head and met his eyes. "I think this was a good idea to do this. I would have never thought to take the time to read up on pregnancy. I was too shocked to believe that I was pregnant."

He flexed her feet and rubbed her calves. "The second best news I've heard all year."

"What was the first?" she asked.

"You leaving Ricky and seeing me," he smirked.

She laughed as she spoke, "I knew you were going to say that."

***

He filled the heart shaped tub and turned on the jet streams. He swished his hand in the water to see if the temperature was just right.

A small red votive candle was at the edge of the tub along with two fluted champagne glasses. The bubbly on ice was sparkling white grape juice.

He extended his hand to hers. "Are you ready to step in?" he asked.

"Yes," she placed her hand in his. She stepped in and leaned back on the left side of the heart. He dropped his boxers, stepped in and relaxed on the right.

She lifted her legs so they could rest on top of his. He caressed them underwater.

"How is it?"

"Lovely," she cooed. She stretched her arms around the sides of the tub. He extended his right hand and reached for her left one. She placed her hand in his.

"What a way to end the year," she said.

While they sat in the warm bubbles, they listened to the TV for the countdown. It was close to midnight.

She asked, "What's your New Year's resolution?"

He answered, "To become closer to God. He answered several prayers this year and provided a few surprises of His own."

"What a wonderful resolution. Mine was to lose weight. I think God had other plans."

"It's getting close," he opened the juice and poured it in the plastic glasses. He held his glass in his left hand and rounded her shoulder with his right one. He leaned in closer to her and raised his glass."

"10-9-8-7-6" was the sound from the TV.

She raised her glass. Her lips were close to his.

"Happy New Year, Love" he breathed and kissed her at the stroke of midnight.

"Happy New Year," she smiled.

CHAPTER 25

They were having a quiet evening at home when the doorbell rang. Carter peeked out of the door pane at Trent Davenport.

Terri rushed up the stairs and hoped she wasn't spotted.

Carter opened the door to meet his friend. "What's going on, frat?" He extended his hand for the secret handshake.

Trent clasped his hand. "I just came by to see if you could help Ricky move.

Carter acted shocked. "I'm sorry to hear that. When is he moving?"

"This weekend."

"I can't, dog. I'm going to be out of town. You okay?"

Trent shuffled his stance and noticed that they were still outside.

"What's up with you? You usually invite me in."

Carter thought fast on his feet. "I'm entertaining."

Trent howled. "You haven't had any in a while. I've got to meet her." Trent moved towards the front door and Carter halted him.

"I'm not introducing her to your lonely horny ass. We'll go out another time and I'll tell you about it."

Trent laughed and allowed Carter his privacy. "Okay, I hear you. Let's plan to get together soon."

"It sounds like a plan to me."

Trent got into his car and left.

Carter went back into the house and called out to her. "He's gone."

She came down the stairs. "That was close. What did he want?"

"He wanted me to help Ricky move."

"Really!" she laughed. "I hope you told him no. How would that look? Sure, I'll help Ricky move. I just moved his wife in my house last week and by the way she's having my baby."

"Come on, Terri." His face was stoic. "It's not funny. I don't know why you married that fool in the first place."

She locked her fingers into his. "We were having problems before we got married. It took almost a year to plan the wedding. By the time all of the families got involved, we knew it was too late to back out of it. I thought it would get better but as you know it didn't."

He blinked his eyes and the expression on his face hadn't changed.

"You're jealous!" she exclaimed.

"Always have been." He stated unapologetically. He put both of his hands on her waist and jerked her towards him. He lowered his eyes and pressed his lips against hers.

She wrapped her arms around his neck and lifted her knee against his thigh. She jerked his shirt up and brushed her fingers up his back.

He whispered in her ear. "I'm glad you're here."

***

Carter was excited about Terri being home with him on a full-time basis.

He called her.

"How's my baby doing? Do you feel any movement yet?"

"Just a flutter. It is too early for anything big."

"I won't be home until later tonight. I'm going to my fraternity meeting and I'm having dinner with some frat brothers. Did you need for me to bring you anything before I get home?"

"I have everything I need. Please enjoy your evening."

"Bye, love."

"Bye."

***

The fraternity meeting was called to order.

Greg and Carter sat together. Ricky was seated near them. Ricky glared at Carter. Greg noted Ricky's stare and warned Carter discreetly.

"I think Ricky is on to you. The brother looks upset."

Carter responded with a bold tone in his voice, "His loss, and my gain. He's not getting her back now."

The fraternity business concluded.

Carter watched as Trent rushed over to Ricky. Greg tapped Carter's shoulder. "Let's go."

Carter stood up and Ricky confronted him.

"What in the hell is my wife doing pregnant and living in your house?"

He sized up Ricky. He would defend his new family. Terri chose to be with him and she's having his baby. "As far as I'm concerned, that's none of your damn business. You aren't with her anymore."

Ricky was enraged. "So how long has she been sleeping with you? That ho couldn't wait for our divorce to get final to fuck you."

Carter bawled up his left fist and hit Ricky directly in the right eye.

Ricky responded with a counter punch, which Carter anticipated and blocked.

He raised his fist to hit Ricky again. He was pulled away before he could deliver the next blow. He jerked and elbowed everyone around him to let him go. He was overpowered and carried backwards.

He looked across the room and saw Ricky being pulled away with his fist drawn ready to continue the fight.

The doors opened, and he was outside and finally allowed to stand on his feet. He was surrounded by six men including Greg. He took deep breaths to calm down and walked in circles to soothe his anger.

"You okay?" asked one of the men.

"Yea, I'm good," he answered in-between breaths.

Greg tugged Carter's sleeve. "Let's go, frat."

Carter glanced back across the parking lot and saw Trent and a few men talking to Ricky. Greg motioned for Carter to follow him to his car. He unlocked the passenger side and waved for Carter to get in.

They arrived at a local bar and settled at their table. The server came by for their order.

Greg flashed a toothy grin. "I'm having the Godfather and my brother is having Jack and Coke. The bill comes to me."

"You don't have to treat, Greg."

Greg waved his hand dismissed him. "Yes, I do. You saved me from punching his ass myself. I owe you dinner too."

Carter laughed.

"You knew that was coming. I don't know what it is about those Dunbar sisters that cause grown men to lose their tempers. Between you and Doug, I don't know who is worse."

"It must be me. At least Doug practiced self-restraint. I couldn't let Ricky get away with that."

The drinks arrived. Carter took a swallow of his Jack and Coke. Terri was his woman and he didn't owe Ricky a damn thing.

Greg halted the server from leaving. "An order of wings for me. You want anything, dog?"

"Yea, I'll have some too." The server grabbed the menus and left.

Greg flicked his wrist and admired at his Rolex. He threw back a swig of his drink. "You and Ricky both slept with the same woman. Hell, his ass was sleeping with Bambi while I was seeing her. Good thing it wasn't serious between her and I, we both would've been kicking his ass."

"Damn, that's right. I almost forgot about that." Carter exclaimed.

"He married her for a reason. Just because they're getting divorced, doesn't mean that he doesn't care about her."

Carter lifted his hand and brushed down his light beard. "He didn't care enough to stay. I'm staying with Terri until she puts me out and she is living in my house. Even then she couldn't get rid of me."

Greg laughed, "I noticed you and Doug both didn't waste any time in getting these women pregnant. Did you think that was going to happen?"

Carter lifted his head back and thought over Greg's question. Terri's pregnancy was unexpected. "I don't know. I had to have her. I had to pick the right moment. I couldn't move too fast or too slow. I made sure that I was available whenever she made the decision to let me in."

Greg sighed with relief, "I'm glad there are no more Dunbar sisters left."

Carter snickered. "What about Maya?"

"Don't start none, won't be none. That sistah hates me." Greg glanced across the room to catch the attention of the server.

"You're next. Don't fight it. It's coming. She's the one." Carter laughed.

"Oh hell naw! Doug tried to jinx me too. You can have them damn Dunbar women. A brother needs his freedom and his sanity." Greg chuckled.

***

Carter composed himself and drove home to be with Terri. She would know from the scrapes on his clothes and bruises on his body that an altercation had ensued. He hoped that she was sleep before he arrived so he could quickly change.

The house was quiet. It was dark except for a small light. He could see his way in without making a disturbance.

He removed all of his clothes and sneaked into the first floor master.

He was in luck.

Terri was already asleep. Carter slid in beside her and she roused. He held her close, squeezed her hand, and gently caressed her stomach. He glided his hand up towards her swollen breasts. She was now awake.

"How was your meeting?"

He kissed her. "It went well. I had dinner with Greg. I didn't mean to come in so late."

"That's okay." Terri rolled over and pulled the covers.

"Terri."

"Uh hmm." she said sleepily.

"I love you."

"I love you too."

CHAPTER 26

He was a happy man. His woman was home waiting for him. Everything was coming together; career, family and the woman he loved. Finally, home from hanging out with Greg. He missed her and was ready to see her.

He walked in and his Nubian queen wasn't happy.

"What's wrong?"

"Do you want to tell me about the fight with Ricky?"

Oh, shit. Who told her?

He shrugged it off and was unapologetic for his behavior. "There's nothing to tell. He made an insult. I proceeded to beat his ass."

She frowned and shouted at him. "The two of you can't go around town beating each other up. You both have careers. What's that going to look like? Both of you having assault and battery charges on your record. You won't be able to get another position anywhere in this country."

He defended his actions. "There are some things that a man won't take."

"What did you do, Carter? I'm beginning to think that it's no accident that I'm here."

"I made myself available to you, Terri."

She put her fingers to her lips and paced the kitchen floor. She wouldn't look at him. Her eyes narrowed and cheeks sucked in. She appeared to be in deep thought.

"Terri, are you okay? Why are you so quiet?" His heart raced, and he couldn't breathe. He couldn't lose her now. He loved her. There was no turning back.

She stopped pacing the floor. "Why did it take me so long to figure this out?"

"Figure what out?" he asked.

Baby, please don't leave me.

She stopped pacing the floor. She stood in front of him with a cold dead stare.

"I'm recalling the events of the past several months and you are correct. You've always been available.

"Before I married Ricky, you seemed to be around more than any of his other friends. I thought it was because the two of you were close. You seemed to talk to me more than you talked to him."

His mouth fell open and he protested. "I was just being friendly."

"Bullshit." She yelled. "You called me or stopped by on nights when Ricky wasn't home. It now seems strange that you would coincidentally have time to see me or call me."

"Terri please…" he pleaded.

I can't lose you.

I love you.

She fumed. "You came by to visit often after I left Ricky. I thought you were just being a concerned friend."

"I was…" he sputtered. " Baby, please don't do this."

Her nostrils flared. "Now I know what started the altercation. Ricky figured out your game and I was too blind to see it."

He was shaken that he was found out. His calculated moves to have Terri were never intended for her to know.

"I-I don't know what you're talking about, Terri." He stammered.

"Oh, you know exactly what I'm talking about. Don't play games with me, Carter. I fully have your number now."

He lowered his head and took a deep breath. It was over. The lies, deceit and dishonesty all blew up in his face. It was time to come clean.

His eyes were downcast for a moment before gazed into her angry face. "Okay, Terri it's true. All of it's true. I wasn't responsible for breaking you and Ricky up. You and Ricky were having problems not related to me. When I met you, I made my move too late. You and Ricky started dating and were inseparable. Then you married him.

"I made every attempt that I could to keep a friendship with Ricky knowing how I felt about you. I called you every chance I could get pretending that I wanted to hang out with Ricky knowing that he was with the woman I should have married first.

"When you left him, I was more than willing to make you forget him. I called you or came by every day to make sure you knew that I was here for you and you didn't need him to come back."

Terri asked, "What about the trip to Savannah?"

"That was planned too. I had to have you. You have no idea how happy I was when you told me you were having my baby."

She stepped back, put her hand to her throat and gasped. Stunned by his revelation, she reached for her purse in the kitchen chair. "I'm not sure that I can do this. I want to be able to trust you."

"Baby, please." He reached for her.

Don't go.

Don't leave me.

She snatched her arm away. "I'm going out for a while."

***

It was very late when she came home. Carter was in the living room watching TV. He heard Terri come in and stood to greet her.

"I see you came home." He focused intently on her face. He didn't want her to be upset with him and would do anything for her affection.

"Yes, I did." Her eyes were cold and hard.

"What do you want me to do?" he asked softly.

She dropped her purse on the couch. "I'm really tired. All I want to do is go to bed."

She went to the bathroom. He sat back down on the couch. He didn't know what to make of her return home. He hoped that she would stay and work things out with him. His only hope was for her to forgive him.

She stood at the end of the couch. He gazed up at her. She still had the angry disappointed expression on her face.

"Are you coming to bed?" she demanded.

He wanted to smile but he knew he was still in the doghouse. She had reservations about their relationship and he hoped their friendship was strong enough to keep them together.

He stood and simply nodded. "Yes, ma'am."

He followed her to their bedroom. Terri was in the bathroom changing when he climbed into bed. She turned out the light and nestled next to him. He cuddled her. She had fallen fast asleep.

***

He woke up early and brewed a pot of decaffeinated coffee early on Sunday morning. He went outside and retrieved the paper. He sat down at the kitchen table and leafed through the news.

He wanted her to see him beyond his deception. He cherished every day waking up with her in his arms. God must truly have forgiven him and he hoped that she would too.

She walked into the kitchen, rubbed her sleepy eyes and yawned. She tightened the belt on her bathrobe. Her hair was under her nightcap and she wore open-toed slippers.

She was beautiful. There was no denying that.

"Good morning." He said and motioned for her to have a seat at the table.

"Good morning." She pulled out a chair and picked up the paper he was reading.

He poured a cup of coffee and microwaved a Krispy Crème doughnut. He placed the doughnut and coffee in front of her.

"Thank you." She sipped the hot drink. He brushed her hair back and kissed her on the cheek slightly in front of her ear.

He sat right beside her and watched as she took a bite of the hot doughnut. "How did you sleep?"

"A little restless. We still have to talk." She sipped her coffee and her eyes remained focused on his.

"I know." He nodded.

"What else are you keeping from me? I want no more secrets."

"I can't think anything else."

She placed her hand on her firm abdomen and rubbed it slowly. He covered his hand over hers. He in leaned close and spoke softly. His lips brushed against her ear.

"You deserve a man who loves you and is faithful to you. Someone who will take care of you. I'm that man."

She removed her hand from under his and picked up her coffee cup with both hands. She took a sip and savored the coffee. She parted her lips as if to speak but he spoke instead.

"Baby, we can do this. I love you. Please."

She squeezed her cup as if she were holding on to it for dear life.

He focused intently on her face. In a desperate appeal, his eyes gazed into hers and silently pleaded for forgiveness.

"Goddammit. Carter." She slammed down her coffee cup. "You make it impossible for me to stay mad at you."

He leaned back in his chair and knew better than to let a smile cross his lips. "Can I do anything for you?"

She stood up and scowled. "Just leave me the hell alone for a while."

He stood up and grabbed her hand before she got away. "I do love you, Terri."

She squeezed his hand and took hold of the free one. The look of frustration was still on her face. "I know. All of this is too fast."

"Not for me. I've waited too long and almost too late."

Carter pressed his lips against hers affirming his desire and passion for her. He held her close feeling each breath she took and the pounding of her heart.

She was unable to resist his charm and she accepted his kiss with all the affection she had for him. He released her, and she whispered to him.

"I love you too."

CHAPTER 27

He was disheartened by the conversation with her parents last week. They weren't thrilled with her decision to move in with him and thought it was too soon.

They also weren't happy with the fact that Terri was still married.

Add an unexpected pregnancy to the list, and that set the tone for a very concerned set of parents who weren't shy about expressing their discontent.

He loved Terri and all they could see was his ruthless pursuit of her.

He'd pressured Terri to move fast in the courtship and wondered if it was too much too soon.

Was she really ready for him?

She'd turned down his proposal several times. He continued to send her flowers occasionally and stopped asking her to marry him for now. He wanted to allow her time to get used to being pregnant as well as living with him.

All of this on his mind made for a restless night. Morning was not far away. Her hand stroked the hairs on his chest and she whispered in his ear. "Good morning."

"Morning."

Maybe everything will be okay.

She twirled a few chest hairs between her fingers. "Can you take off Friday? I have somewhere I'd like to go for the weekend."

Startled by her request he answered, "Yea. I'll put in a day's vacation when I get to work. Where do you want to go?"

"It's a surprise. Just take the day off and we'll take it from there."

He yawned and glanced over at the clock. The alarm was set to go off in about twenty minutes.

She kissed his neck below his beard and brushed her hand between his thighs.

"Breakfast?" he asked in his smooth sultry voice.

"Absolutely." She wrapped her fingers around his shaft.

"We've got eighteen minutes."

***

It was 6:00 a.m. when Carter packed the bags in the car for their trip. Terri wanted to get on the road early and beat the rush hour traffic in Atlanta.

She was in the car when he got in. He was ready to pull out of the driveway. "Why won't you tell me where we're going?"

She shrugged. "Because it is a surprise. Did you bring all of the groceries?"

"I did. Do you want me to drive?" he asked.

"Yes, I'll give you the directions." She fastened her seatbelt.

There wasn't much conversation other than the directions for each turn. When they got closer to their destination, he recognized where they were going.

"This is the cabin we stayed in for New Year's!" he said excitedly. A huge smile swept across his face.

"That's right," she snickered. "I wanted to make sure this particular one was available."

After picking up the keys from the reservation office, they drove to the cabin. He parked the car and kissed her. "Don't touch anything. I'll bring everything in."

After they settled in the cabin, she beckoned him to sit at the kitchen table. "I rented the cabin so that we could sit and talk. You really seemed distant this week and I wanted to find out why."

"After talking with your parents, I realized that I was putting you under a lot of pressure. I knew that I was smothering you with my feelings, so I decided to pull back."

She pointed her finger at him. "Don't you ever pull back on your feelings for me! I could tell the difference all week. I would rather have you smother me than not to feel you at all."

He was surprised by this revelation. He thought that she would appreciate the space. The fact was she didn't want space.

His face beamed with joy. "Oh, I have no problem with releasing my feelings for you if you have no problem accepting them."

She reached across the table and placed her hand in his and squeezed it. "I love the way you express yourself to me. Don't ever change."

His eyes glazed, and a smile eased across his face. "I could sit here with you for the next fifty years. Raise a family, have children, and lots of grandchildren."

She smiled and nodded. "We haven't talked much about the baby, our plans and what we could do to change the world."

He raised up from his chair and knelt beside her. He placed his hand over her abdomen and caressed it. "We've been under a lot of stress. Most of that is behind us. Our baby will be very blessed to have us as parents."

She placed her hand over his. "I never gave motherhood a second thought. It was in the back burner. I really wanted to start my restaurant."

"Do it," he said. "You still can. Having a baby doesn't stop your dream. We'll work it out. I offered before, and the offer still stands. Put together a business plan and I'll help."

"I know you will."

He squeezed her hand. "I mean it. Who knows? I may become a partner. It may become so successful that you have a chain of restaurants. I believe in you and it's time you believed in yourself."

Her lips parted. "I don't know what to say. I love you so much. How did I miss you the first time around?"

He chuckled. "We're together now and that's what's important."

"It is," she agreed and wrapped her arms around his neck. "The plans start after my divorce is final."

***

The smell of bacon woke him up from his slumber. He rubbed his eyes, put on his boxers and followed the smell to the kitchen.

"I've got coffee started," she said.

"I'll get the cups," he said. He pulled them from the dishrack and placed them on the table.

"I made bacon and eggs. I've been craving that a lot lately." She broke off a small piece and fed it to him.

He held her wrist and licked the bacon taste off her finger. "Good bacon."

She laughed. "Thank you. I thought that I would take you for a walk this morning. As you know, I can't go far. I must stay near the bathroom,"

"Do you want to go after we eat?" he asked.

"After our showers."

He nodded and agreed.

After breakfast was finished, and the kitchen cleaned. The pair dressed for the day. They left the cabin fifteen minutes later.

He brought the camping chairs and a backpack. She carried a thermos filled with coffee. They found a clearing by the lake not far from where they were the last time they came for New Year's.

He set up the chairs, walked over by the lake, and enjoyed the view. He extended his hand for her to stand by him.

"Well," she breathed. "A lot has changed this year. I would've never predicted a divorce, a new man in my life and a baby."

"Yes, a lot has changed. Thank you for bringing me back here. It was a nice surprise."

She squeezed his hand. "I didn't bring you here by accident, it was planned."

He laughed. "You're starting to plan now? Are you picking up some of my traits?"

She reached for his other hand. He faced her, gazed down into her eyes, and waited for her to speak.

"Yes, I wanted to bring you someplace special." The cool crisp air rustled through the trees. The smell of a wood fire infused the air.

"You did, why is that?" Carter asked.

Her face glowed with contentment. "I wanted to know what your thoughts were on a spiritual and physical commitment. This would involve being a husband and father. This commitment would last for a lifetime and it involves love, trust and honesty. Would you be interested in a commitment like that?"

Carter loosened his hold on her and realized what she said. "Are you asking me to marry you?"

She peacefully nodded. "Yes, I am. I am so in love with you. Are you ready to marry me?"

"I am." He kissed her with every emotion in his soul. God truly blessed him for a lifetime.

ABOUT THE AUTHOR

MIA MAE LYNNE - has enjoyed writing from the time she was in grade school. She started a diary and wrote in the journal for seven years. She always knew that one day all her creative ideas would come into fruition and writing has been her escape.

"The Chronicles of Fate" series was born in the metro Atlanta area allowing her to explore her creative side. The series was later renamed to "Southern Men Don't Fall in Love" with "Atlanta's Most Eligible Bachelor" as the first book in the series with many more to follow. She has enjoyed writing the series and has embraced each of the characters as they have entrusted her with their stories to share with the world.

After discovering psychic and mediumship abilities, she became a student of spiritualism. She has newly begun this path and has explored the traditional areas of tarot, numerology, astrology and other related areas of interest in the metaphysical arts. She has received training from the Fellowship of the Spirit in New York as well as read numerous books and attended various classes to expand her knowledge.